BORROWED TIME

HASSAN DAOUD

Borrowed Time

Translated from the Arabic by
Michael K. Scott

TELEGRAM
London San Francisco Beirut

First published as *Ayyaam Zaa'idah* by Dar al-Jadid, 1990
This English translation published in 2008 by Telegram

ISBN: 978-1-84659-047-4

Manufactured in Lebanon

TELEGRAM
26 Westbourne Grove, London W2 5RH
825 Page Street, Suite 203, Berkeley, California 94710
Tabet Building, Mneimneh Street, Hamra, Beirut
www.telegrambooks.com

Glossary

Aya kabeera the 'Great Verse of the Qur'an'; '*inna fatahna laka fathan mubeenan*' is the opening line of surah 48, *al-fath* ('Victory'): 'Verily we have given you a glorious victory.'

Ashrafiyah a historic residential area of East Beirut.

Ayat verses of the Qur'an within a chapter or '*surah*'.

Azraa'eel the Angel of Death mentioned in the Qur'an.

Bab Edriss 'Edriss Gate', a landmark retail and business area in Beirut in what is generally referred to as the city's downtown.

Dar 'house' in Arabic, sometimes also meaning a high-ceilinged 'living room' in a traditional urban Levantine house, often partitioned from the rest of the central portion of the house by columns and archways. In the South Lebanon rural context of this novel, it refers to an entire enclosed or walled-in property, including garden, terraces, patios, *mastabas*, and any residential or other structures.

Debbas Square in Beirut's heyday, a famous commercial and transportation hub.

Franji 'French' (or 'Frenchy'); more generally the denoting of Western, non-indigenous style or mode. Foreign.

Hajj   denotes in a familiar yet respectful manner a man who has been on the pilgrimage to Mecca that is one of the five obligatory 'pillars' of the Islamic faith. *Hajja* is the feminine form. This title becomes almost inseparable from the person, such is the degree of respect it bestows. Literally: 'pilgrim'.

Halwa   in the West known as 'Halva', a sweet confection made from sesame seeds and sugar and molded into blocks. It can be studded with pistachio or other nuts and is usually sliced to eat with bread.

Husseiniyah   a mosque, in Shi'ite Islam, which also provides a place specifically used for the preparation of bodies for funerals; named after Hussein the martyred and revered son of the fourth caliph Ali.

Ibreeq   a traditional clay or glass water jug with a thin neck and a small spout providing a manageable stream of water down through the air into the mouth of a person holding the *ibreeq* aloft.

'Id   holiday, or celebration, both secular and religious. In this context, one of two major Islamic feasts.

Ka'ak   a salty-sweet bread ring with sesame and spices.

Khamseen   literally, a 'fifty-dayer', for the hot easterly (in the Levant and Palestine) wind that brings dust from the Arabian desert, usually in the spring.

Labneh   a strained yoghurt cheese popular throughout Lebanon, particularly as an item on the breakfast menu. eaten with olives and bread.

Marwaniyah   a village in South Lebanon, in the 'Jabal Aamel' (Mount Aamel) area which is nestled between the South Lebanese coastal plain to the east and the south-western tip of the Bekaa Valley, to the west.

Mastaba   traditional solid, low, stone retaining wall, often used as a seating area, surrounding a rural stone or mud-brick house. Here, it indicates a slightly raised stone platform built as a foundation and upon which the house is centered, allowing one to walk outside and around the house itself, somewhat above the level of the ground.

Minbar   the pulpit from which the Imam delivers the Friday Prayer in a mosque or Husseiniyah.

Muezzin   the person who performs the *adhaan*, the ritual call to prayer, from the minaret of a mosque.

Nabatiyah   the largest inland town and the administrative seat of Jabal Aamel; also a major center of commerce and cottage industries; and site of the annual religious commemoration of the martyrdom of Hussein.

Sanaaye'   a residential district and public park near the West Beirut shopping district of Hamra. It was generally spared the destruction wrought by the Lebanese civil war on the old 'downtown' areas to the east, such as Debbas and Bab Edriss.

Sayyid   an honorific title given to a man descended from the Prophet.

Sherwaal   traditional baggy pants worn by peasantry in rural Lebanon, drawn tight at the waist and ankles, usually black and made of thick cotton.

Tarboosh   a fez, the conical red felt rimless and tassled hat worn by gentlemen of means, especially during Ottoman times.

Tatkheeti   a confined storage room or space, stretching horizontally (like a '*takht*' – bed or stage) and inserted above the ceiling of a room, usually a kitchen; a kind of half-attic.

I

My I.D. card shows I'm now ninety-four, with a picture of me aged forty stuck on it. For years I claimed I was actually three years younger, as my father registered my birth to match the age of boys I know were not my generation, to get me out of military service. Ten or twenty years ago, if I said this, some men – my sons among them – would respond that on the contrary, I'm in fact three years older than the document indicates, in keeping with my father claiming I was too young to serve. And they would tell stories putting me in the same generation as Abu Ali Youssef and Hajj Ali Farhat. I know that couldn't be true since they were off on their first trip to Palestine when I was not old enough to be left alone with the cows. Then they'd talk about events that took place when I was already an old man, with Ali Farhat confidently confirming what they were saying. That's because our evenings together, during the years before his death, had got him thinking that we were always peers, friends of the same generation. These people were adamant about my age. They considered my anecdotes from those days to be too few and unchanging, insufficient to swerve them from their thinking. Whenever they picked up talking they'd carry on parroting what they'd grown so used to hearing themselves say. Eventually, I realized it was pointless to argue with them, to tell the two or three stories that were the only ones I held to be true.

Now, I can't even recall things that happened much later in my life. The picture of the interior of the bakery that I took over in Bab Edriss is no longer suspended in my mind's eye, so that in place of its iron racks and shelving I see an assortment of counters and displays from other bakeries – some not even mine. I'll set a remembered foot on the polished marble of my bakery's front doorstep only to discover suddenly that I'm really in brother Hajj Salim's bakery, the one he took over in Ras Beirut the year of the big 'Khamseen'. I'd also see myself on that heavy chair where Hajj Salim would always motion for me to sit so he could talk to me, all the while selling bread and chatting with his workers. I felt sorry for him, starting work at an age well over fifty.

I didn't go on telling those two or three stories of mine. Before cutting them out completely I would delete something from them, some word or detail, and the next time I'd cut something else – until I could just remind them about it in a brief word or two. I'd start up with a loud, rising voice that would then suddenly die out. As if I admitted not just three but – let's add up all this disputed time – *six* years, for them to have me reach an age no one in the family ever reached. I began to keep quiet whenever they started talking about people's ages. Of late I've begun to mix the days up in front of them, putting the visit of one of my children three or four days later than it was – so that they have to correct me and say that it happened the day before yesterday and not last Friday. Every time this happens their conviction grows that I am indeed three years older than my I.D. card says. So call it six years, all told. Just as if I had fallen into a pit, six full years deep. I go along and I bow to them, because I'm losing the strength to stick to my true age. It requires a tenacity and stubbornness I no longer possess.

They don't even accept in compromise the age suggested by the I.D. card, which, ever since I gave up arguing with them, I came to accept as my real age. When one of my grandchildren comes for a visit I give him the I.D. card to look at. He examines the picture and asks me about the bakery in Debbas Square – which, in the last days of its operation, I thought of as something only remotely related to me, rather like those three uncles of mine who went about distributing their photo- graphs to all the relations in the family. I always reply with the same few words I used on his last visit. Then he'll ask other questions and I'll repeat the answers I gave before, and he'll think that I don't know anything beyond this.

Once, cousin Hajj Youssef raised his voice against a stranger who came and went around our village begging. He didn't like what I had given the man and recited some harsh words from the Qur'an to me. I didn't know how to respond. Hajj Youssef yelled in the man's face and repeated those same words from the Qur'an, as if he were cursing him.

I don't talk and don't remember. I can see how people who don't like talking don't know how to remember. My cousin

Hajj Youssef would always tell me stories about our house, about my father, about his wife my 'auntie', and about many men who are now dead. And he is younger than I am.

They'll never come around to admitting my true age from my I.D. card. They'll even take a month and turn it into a year. Between one visit and the next someone will add a year to my life. They add on the years in proportion to the amount of time they are away from me. For some of my grandchildren I am ninety-five and for others I am ninety-seven. They're in a hurry for me to reach 100. I know this, so I say to them that it isn't right for me to be left alone with no one to cook for me when I turn 100. Now, they lower their heads when they pass my window so I can't see them climb up the stairs to their family on the floor above me. I see them when I'm lying on my elevated bed, with the mattress flush against the windowsill. I shout out at whoever is on the stairs and he'll come to me and say he thought I was asleep and didn't want to wake me. I'll remain lying on my bed. Just two minutes and he will go – the same boy I gave 100 pounds for a haircut.

I've never known anyone who reached 100. Folks claim Abu Muhammad Nassim did, but I know for a fact that he wasn't even ninety when he died. His family added years to his age over time, and when they found him dead on the terrace they added seven more right then and there, proclaiming him 107 years old. No, I don't know anyone who's made it to 100. I often wonder what it will be like if I make it to this age that no one I've known ever has. Before, years ago, I'd ponder men older than myself, wondering what I would be like in, say, ten years. As if by doing so I could learn how to enter into ages I didn't yet know.

I'm now in my ninety-forth year. I live in the house I built in the old days. It's right up against this big one-room house that belonged to my father. They left his place empty after two of the tree trunks that held up its roof rotted away and the roof started to sag, and bring bits of dirt down onto the floor. I told my son Qassem that it was going to cave in before he could tile the roof and put a heavy water fountain in the middle of the floor upstairs. He paid me no mind and built his house over it, right across from me. His wife, who stopped taking care of me some time ago now, looks down at me from up there on their balcony, as if she is counting the seconds until someone arrives to tend to me – while I go about filling the water jug, or washing my clothes on the *mastaba*, or as I try, shaking and trembling, to dispose of the hot water in a pot in which I have just boiled an egg.

The late Fatima never let on a thing, right up to the day before she died. That's when I went to her bedside to ask forgiveness for anything I may have done to her, saying: 'Forgive me, Fatima'. But she turned her head away. I asked her again, but she still wouldn't shift her head from the edge of her pillow. I wasn't able to soften my voice the way so many did as they watched her lying there in my father's ancient room. When my wife approached her and also said: 'Forgive me, Fatima', she paid it no mind. I left the darkened room with a lingering image of the big tumor under the skin of her neck. In her last days she would stand in front of the windowpane staring at us as we ate. I would shout out to Khadija: 'Tell

13

her to cover up her tumor.' Its fine blue veins were like those on a cow's stomach. I was only in my seventies then so I could see her in the dim light. In those days I would go to the threshing floor with a big sack cloth in one hand and a winnow in the other and I'd single-handedly fill the barn with hay in two days.

My legs were still strong when I first got cataracts. I refused to go to the hospital. My grown boys took me by force. Qassem, the middle one, raised his voice at me and shoved me into the car. I stumbled as I went down the four steps to the courtyard. I knew that disease would strike my legs and my body. The demise of every man I've known started as a weakness in one area of their bodies.

Hajj Abdel Latif, a man in our village, always stands straight and strong with his eyes full of whiteness, swaying his head left and right, as if this will trap the disease in his head, and prevent it from descending to the rest of his body. He shakes his head the whole time while squeezing the hands of whoever he greets and speaks with his Beirut accent, which makes him seem smiling and happy. I pushed away the image of Hajj Abdel Latif in the car on the way to hospital because he and his relatives were different from other people in the village, making it impossible for me to be like him. Those who do not live as we live, do not die as we die. In my contemplation of men who were ten or twenty years older than me I would try not to allow the image of Hajj Abdel Latif's face to come to mind for very long, since he seemed to pass through life differently than everyone else. Hajj Abdel Latif is not like me. Rather, the men who squat in the sunshine on their houses' *mastabas* are like me. Raising their eyes towards me and rejoicing in their laziness and warmth, they seem like the men of old from the stories my cousin Hajj Youssef told.

I would pass by them in a hurry on the way back home from the threshing floors. It's enough for me to recall their fathers to know how I will be. I know that my standing among them screaming and shouting will not set me apart from them. It won't change a thing that I went down into the well when I was seventy, while the other men holding my rope waited for me around the mouth of the well, fearful. I always knew I would end up like them.

Not like Hajj Abdel Latif, then, but maybe like blind Hajja Zahiya, sitting by herself in her room at the bottom of the terrace, under my house, who would go about feeling for the path to the open-air toilet with her feet, and turning her head in all directions as if she could see, before dropping her garments and squatting, revealing the flesh of her white and wrinkled bottom. What I see streaming from her in the moment before I turn my face away recalls the ways of the old-timers of Hajj Youssef's stories.

I still speak with the accent I picked up from people in Beirut, though it is not the same accent that Hajj Abdel Latif has, ending his sentences with those smiles that make him appear more like the women. He is talkative like they are too and, like them, he likes to sit at home for long hours with his son and the neighbors and his water-pipe. When their cars arrive the neighbors hurry to join up with them and while away the evening in their company, men and women coming from various houses nearby. Hajj Abdel Latif sits them down all around him, and he sets about conversing with them in that cool accent of his that highlights the whiteness of his face and his limbs.

My daughter Bahija stands tall like a man when she comes to visit me at home. She doesn't stay longer than the time required to ask after my health and place the food she has prepared for me into the pantry. She stands a while in the courtyard deliberately casting her eyes about the dried-up plants around the water basins, pretending to prolong the time spent with me. I don't get up from my bed, but remain stretched out on it waiting for her to leave, so that I can cast the blanket off and lower my feet to the ground. When she brings her husband they stay an even shorter while. One of them will enter through the door and flip the light switch, and then tidy up my medicines, place my clock and my pack of tobacco and the myriad other things spread around the bed, the top of the heater and the couch, putting everything onto the table. Then he will open the window so the smell and stale air can escape.

I don't find anything to say on these short visits. My daughter Bahija doesn't allow me the time to remember her when she was a little girl in the house, so I speak to her as if she was one of her grown brothers. After all, she talks about things the way they do. Abu Fayez, my eldest son, preoccupies himself with tidying up the room when he comes. He will reorganize things in it several times so that there is no time for us to talk. I see him bend his big and heavy body over to pick up little scraps of bread. He is breathless from his age and his weight. I say: 'Sit down, Abu Fayez', and he increases

his shifting and twisting about. When I start to complain
and moan about my pain, he'll say I need to get over my fear
of death, grumbling and scolding me, avoiding eye contact,
like he intends his words for someone else. None of them are
interested in hearing anything more than answers relating to
questions about my health, never expecting me to say more
than 'Fine, thanks be to God'. They ask me how I feel, so I
respond with what is expected of me and say: 'Praise God'.
The whole time they're standing there frowning so as to ward
off any complaint I might have about my insomnia or the
coldness in my limbs when I go out to pee in the night –
something I started to dread even before Hajja Khadija passed
away. She slept in the second room with the photograph of
my dead grandchildren hanging on the wall. I knew she feared
going to sleep the way I did when she turned the bed around
all on her own so that her eyes wouldn't fall on that picture.
She'd sit on the edge of the bed by herself with her eyes closed,
waiting for sleep to weigh them down, while I listened to that
sound she made, a sound like something coming from the
stomachs of cats. I would say to her, 'Come on, let's stay up
late tonight, Hajja!' She would take up the same position in
Hajj Ali Farhat's home, raising her head and closing her eyes
in front of Hajja Miriam sitting sick on her bed, while Hajj
Ali Farhat and I were busy rolling cigarettes and spitting away
the bits of tobacco that clung to our tongues.

We started to spend every evening with them at their
house, one of us going ahead and the other following a short
while later. I felt in those days as if we were at the end of our
lives, since we were doing the same things every day. We'd

talk about our children in Beirut, Hajj Ali Farhat and I, and he would start the evening off by boiling tea for us. In their house I was kind to Hajja Khadija, whom I could see dozing off, and who would then get up when I got up. I felt I was close to her there, and would feel pity towards her because she was at the end of her life. But I'd quickly forget all that when we returned home. I'd shout out at her from my room, to go and get some water for me, and she would pass by the door in front of me with those cat sounds rising from her, a monotonous whining that she thought I couldn't hear. And then I would shout at her once again and she would suddenly hurry up, as if someone had pushed her from behind. But the whining went on and on as she poured the water from the water jug.

I never lowered my voice, and Hajja Khadija went on fearing it until she died. I would push her into my room to sweep, and she'd go about swatting the floor lightly with the broom. We only spoke in our two rooms, separated by the door that Hajja Khadija closed every time she passed over its threshold. I used to shout at her, demanding to know what she was doing over there in her room. Whenever I went in to get something from my closet, which I kept in there with her, I noticed that her room smelled different from mine. I thought it was from the old string of black beads on her long rosary, but it didn't get into the things in my closet, which I kept under lock and key. I would exit and shut the door behind me, just as she did, since I didn't like to see her stripping or changing her clothes. Hajja Khadija never dirtied her clothes and never wore them out. It was as if nothing ever came out of her body, a body that economized on its outlay. She intended to distribute that over a longer life. The clothes hung in her closet for twenty or thirty years, including the black coat that reminded me of her younger self. As for me, my shirtsleeves and collars were always frayed and disintegrating when I attended their funerals.

I cried for Hajja Khadija. Everyone saw me wiping my tears with the palm of my hand, tapping her tomb with my cane as I told her: 'You've died and left me alone, Hajja.' They saw my thin body and figured I wouldn't last long, so weak and diminished I must have appeared. But a change came over me when I got home.

They thought I was going to die the day they buried my daughter. Her three sons sat on the Husseiniyah's mourning chairs and cried through their father's recitation of Qur'anic verses from the pulpit, like he does for all the dead. The many years haven't brought us any closer; in passing I would greet him as if he were just a distant relation of hers. Sitting there in the Husseiniyah the thought occurred to me that I had kept my daughter all those years with a man I did not know. He mouthed the *ayat* like a man imitating someone else, contorting his lips. He isn't close to me, and neither are his three sons with the cheeks that bellow out when they cry. To me, they are like workmen from some other town.

My trips to the cemetery started getting more frequent when I stopped going down to Beirut. I didn't cry over my brother Hajj Salim. He was my neighbor at home, with nothing but a narrow line of concrete, the exact placement of which we often squabbled over, marking our properties. It got to the point that I was about to demolish his *mastaba* wall because he built it a meter into my land. My voice would ring out at him as I sat at the door to my room, and he would answer from his *mastaba* in that vile taunting voice of his. We nearly came to blows; in the end, my sons said we should be ashamed – two old men fighting like little boys. I didn't cry over his grave, and afterwards I continued talking about him as if he were alive. Sayyid Mahdi told me that time only makes brothers hate each other more. Sayyid Mahdi clothes his entire family in old sheikhs' cloaks handed down for generations, which make the son look like the father and brother like brother. So how could it be otherwise for Hajj Salim and me, who had nothing in common and looked as if we were men from two different families?

It's not our sharing the house that put a distance between us. My brother Mahmoud, who lived far from us, wasn't any closer to me. I couldn't see much difference between him and the neighbors he chose to live amongst. The thing is: I didn't run into him as much as I did Hajj Salim. When we did meet, he would talk to me about our mother and father. We'd amble about the terraces together, walking over the dried-up land that was now divided amongst us, and he'd complain to me about his ailments, usually bringing the conversation around to how things were when we were two small boys at home with Father. But that didn't have much of an impact on me; on leaving the dusty terraces I never knew what I should feel towards him. He always seemed a stranger among us. In Beirut, whenever my sons invited him to their homes for a meal, he would sit silently the whole time, unsure what to do.

'Get up, Abu Mustafa', I'd shout. His eyes would widen and then his voice would fail.

So I didn't cry the day they buried him either. I didn't even go to his house to pay my respects after people scattered away from the cemetery. I went home with my sons. I didn't cry at any of my relative's funerals, and over the passage of time I grew more and more indifferent and distant from them. There was nothing left of the closeness that I could see in those photos of my three uncles, which they passed around to everyone in the family. I saw those photos in every house I entered, shining under the glass frames that encased them. 'They party together every night', Hajja Amina, Hajj Salim's wife, said. They were elderly in those pictures, making our children think the three of them had died all together on the same day. Sheikh Mahmoud, his head tilting to the side from the weight of his turban, looked as if he was listening to his two wide-eyed brothers who appeared to sense that Sheikh Mahmoud was no longer a well-known scholar in the villages, and had become simply their brother again, nothing more.

People distributed the photographs all around, reuniting the split-apart family, and men would make the rounds visiting their relatives almost as if they were counting heads. They leave one house only to enter another, talking nicely about uncle's youngest daughter, the poor one, so that she might not appear to anyone to be like the poor women who lived near her house.

The photos suggested the three spent years in a conviviality that they carried into each other's home. Even my youngest uncle, whom I knew to be furious with his brothers, looked quiet and self-effacing in the picture, in which his head is lower than their two heads. They appear side by side against the wall, as if their father had bequeathed to them such a posture, forty years before his death. It was he who would walk out ahead if there was a feud with another family. He walked in front, his rifle in his hand, and they would follow him holding clubs and heavy rakes. In the house at the entrance to the village, where the whole family would meet, he alone would go out to meet whoever was there to fight them, standing on the side of the path. Sheikh Mahmoud, who had not yet started to wear a turban, was the most miserable of the three brothers, since he had kept raining blows with his heavy stick on Ali Bayram's back until he killed him. Sheikh Mahmoud was always two men in my mind: a man pounding on Ali Bayram's back; and a man tilting his head under his turban and speaking softly and slowly, full of sympathy for the women married to his brothers and his cousins. Two different men that only a photograph could render as one. For he, with his sleepy eyes that seemed on the verge of tears, looked as if he regretted having done something he was forced to do by his brothers.

I knew very well how they had lived, but still I was innocently seduced by the photograph. I saw their demeanor in this photograph to be their essential nature, something unblemished by fraternal differences and squabbles. I loved photographs. I had a picture of myself taken when I was forty – the one used on my I.D. card – but I also had a large print of it made. I framed it in gold and hung it in my Debbas Square bakery.

Despite the cataracts, I never went blind. In the car, back

from Beirut, my sons Qassem and Nayef sat quietly in the
front. Whenever the car turned a corner I would ask them
where we were, trying to get them to say something. I asked
them to adjust the bandages because they were drooping from
my eyes. They helped me out of the car, but I didn't head for
the house; instead I paused after every step, forcing them to
put me back on the right path.

When they brought me glasses I didn't know how to put
them on. They were thick and heavy, and whenever someone
entered through the wide house gate I would raise my head
and stick my shoulders back in order to make out who it was.
The visitor would think that I didn't see them, and would turn
quickly towards the stairs of Hajj Salim's house. I don't know
what I must have looked like to them. To me I looked old and
bizarre. I tried to imagine how Hajja Khadija would look if
I put glasses on her face, or Hajj Ali Farhat, or even my boys,
with their hair covering their big heads. Hajja Khadija gave my
children her thick hair, which made my elder daughter's face
look thin and sick years before they took her off to Beirut.

Yes, the glasses made me look very strange, so I wound
scraps of cloth around the sides to stop them from shining
on my old wrinkled face. 'Why are you doing that, Father?'
Qassem asked. 'So the sides don't hurt my ears', I replied.

Not only did I not go blind, I also didn't get struck with
what hit the white-eyed Hajj Abdel Latif. The flesh around his
eyes had thickened and sagged, revealing the veins of his tear
ducts, as if they were bits of his intestines. Those are the old
kinds of illnesses, from the times when symptoms appeared on
faces and bodies. No girl nowadays will be born with a tumor

like the one Fatima had between her neck and her chest. These things only happen as a result of the chaotic lives the people before us lived. I'd see her in front of me and lower my eyes to her bare feet, noticing her untrimmed toenails, sending a silent signal for her to get out of my way. She watched us through the window-panes as we ate so I shouted out to my wife to stop eating. I called out, 'Forgive me, Fatima', but she turned her face away. I knew she kept in her mind the memory of my driving her to the terraces by the force of my voice and my shouting at her and at her sister.

The people sitting with me change their positions and their manner of talking when I pull the glasses off my eyes and put them in my vest pocket. They think that I see them differently from behind the thick specs. I say to my daughter-in-law, to infuriate her, that Azraa'eel, the Angel of Death, cannot touch me. She goes upstairs silently and doesn't start her muttering until she gets to the carved railing in front of her house. Then she'll mutter on and on as she walks through all of the rooms. Her hatred for me pushes her almost against her will into moving between the wardrobes and the beds, as if she doesn't know how to stop her body from ricocheting all over the place – and her ranting only aggravates her movements and her turmoil.

She could not conceal her joy when my illness intensified and they'd walk me to the village square and wait for the car to come and take me to Nabatiyah. She'd come out in a tizzy, adjusting the outdoor clothing she threw upon herself in a rush, and she'd look worn out. But she wouldn't look at me. And when I shouted out in pain she continued talking to neighbors who gathered just a few paces away. She distracted them from me, thinking they would exacerbate my illness, which she assumes (every time) will be my last.

I understood that her silence and composure would not return until they brought me back from Nabatiyah and she saw me walking up the dusty trail from the car to the house unaided, carrying my medicines. The square would be empty of everyone when I returned. And when I go out to the *mastaba* and sit on my collapsing old chair, I know that they will have all dispersed to their homes with their doors locked. It will be bright, brilliant sunlight outside while they sit silently in their darkened houses. Houses I always assumed empty until a child emerged from the door, or a woman walked silently to the clothesline.

II

I'm in my ninety-fourth year now. My house, which I don't leave these days, isn't any dirtier than before my wife died. After her death I discovered that housework doesn't take much time. I take care of it in a few minutes each day before sitting down to deal with my boredom. I sweep up the dust, dried leaves, and scraps of bread into a pile behind the door, the way Hajja Khadija did.

All the things scattered around the house I left in their places. The Hajja wasted a lot of time by placing things that go together far apart. I ended up like her, moving from the pantry to the kitchen and then to the tea cupboard, still in her room, to make some tea. And like her I leave the tea cups, sticky with sugar, on the edge of the upper-level *mastaba*. I would shout at her whenever I saw the tea cups there, and she would come over and put them somewhere else.

I used to see the *ibreeq*, the water jug, coated with calcium deposits on the inside and get irritated without saying anything to her. I knew it was a kind of filth that water cannot clean, because the calcium adheres to the glass and penetrates it. I used to think water jugs were spoiled by prolonged use, but when I saw shiny *ibreeqs* in other people's homes I knew our house must have been completely covered in some insoluble dirt. The white sheets and pillows on top of the sofas and beds appeared heavy with dried dust nestled deep in their weave.

At times when I sit in my chair at sunset, and become wistful about Hajja Khadija, I think, 'This is how old people's homes are, they are never cleaned', and I turn my head to look for her and see her sitting there on the edge of the bed, silent. I get even more wistful, so I get up from my chair and walk in front of the door to her room, hoping my footsteps might get her moving more energetically, and she might think there is someone moving around in the house.

I kept all the things exactly as they were, in their places, and moved about them the same way she did. I even wash my plate where she stood, in the narrow space next to the *mastaba*. I pour some water and swish it around, letting it drip down onto the concrete floor that extends to the edge of the courtyard terrace. The water splatters onto the surrounding dirt and onto the door of the bathroom that I built a long time ago. That's what Hajja Khadija would do, oblivious of the smell of the dirty water. So I do the same thing now and, as long as I am alone, do not feel ashamed of the odor.

I don't drip clean water on the dirty surface of the concrete floor. Hajja Khadija would wash the filth off our children's children and the suds would leak out from the little bathroom. There would be a white liquid froth emerging from the bathroom and tracing a narrow well-worn course. Their voices would rise out of the interior of the bathroom because she would wash them all together. When one would come out naked and dripping, I would shout at him to run to the room. We were still in our seventies, and they would send us the children from Beirut. I would let them sleep in my room because they were afraid of the darkness in Hajja Khadija's room. When they woke up in the morning the laughing would start of its own accord, as if someone had been making them laugh in their dreams.

It wasn't just the dirty water, but also my pissing. I would aim my pee, once my thighs were stuck securely in the wide openings of the verandah railing, but it would end up sprinkling all over. The smell of it in the morning would be worse, and no amount of dirty dishwater would get rid of it, even if I rinsed the dishes twice a day.

The children also left things in their places after the death of Hajja Khadija. They didn't move her bed back to the ancient room that had been my father's house. They kept it in its place under the pictures of my daughter and my dead grandchildren. I didn't ask anymore why it was kept made up with all of the sheets, pillows, and bedspread when no one was ever going to sleep in it. They cram a good many families upstairs in the rooms of the building's top three floors, and I sleep alone in the same amount of space that they all crowd into. I don't call them, since I knew they would either be afraid of sleeping in a house in which many dead people have been washed, or they would be disgusted with the traces of me on the bedcovers.

I'm alone by myself in the house – they think my many years have made me familiar with death, unafraid of it. Or they might think that my many years have enabled me to know death, just by existing on its edge. They think of the names of people long since deceased, the ones I know and the ones I never knew, and figure that I must know death and that it must not hold any terror for me – since I am such an ancient one, someone of the same generation as death itself. But at other times they don't believe that I am moaning from my pain.

Abu Fayez told me to get over my fear of death. He said that hastily and scornfully, as if he was pushing me to cut out my complaining. I climb up to them in the evening and sit among them as if I had come as a guest. They'll say very little when I arrive, and become preoccupied with whatever they were discussing before I came up. I'll say to my eldest, 'Pass me the *ibreeq*, son', and he will get up from the group and bring me the *ibreeq*. I choose him in particular because I remember a time when he knew me and did not know them. He recognizes that, and says to me, 'Here, Father', and continues standing in front of me until I have finished drinking.

There are many of them in their house, and when I get up to leave someone always takes me to the head of the stairs and no further. Only their brother-in-law slept downstairs in my quarters. They forced him into doing it, slamming the door behind him, like trapping a rat that wandered inside. I pointed with my cane where he could get the bed sheets, blanket, and pillow. I knew he wouldn't want to sleep on Hajja Khadija's bed. He lifted the bedding cautiously with both his hands, as if knowing he wouldn't sleep in it.

I know the children left everything in its place because they thought that, in the time I had left, it wouldn't be worth redecorating the house. I don't disagree. I carry around a sticky sugar bowl and leave the cupboard door open. I don't do anything to clean up the dirt that falls from the roof of my father's room. I am someone who rented houses in Beirut and lived in them as if only trying them out. I would take a house and then leave it before I had gotten to know it. I don't even remember the number of rooms in the house in Sanaaye', the one I left for my youngest daughter. I would arrive there late in the evening and leave again before anyone was awake. They would wait for me in their cotton shirts with their shoulders and chests showing, and I would share no news from my day at work. I always saw them as little children, even after they had married and had children of their own. They didn't change anything about themselves; they seemed to believe that nothing could entertain them more than just sitting together recollecting the things they did when they were little.

I didn't linger among them, knowing they came to laugh amongst themselves, so I always got up. My daughter Nayefa always waited for me to fall asleep before closing the door and rejoining the party until the wee hours. In the mornings I remember they would come to the bakery late and tired-out. So I would put the heavy bread boards on their heads and press down on them to make them stand up straighter. They were lazy and phlegmatic, and all they knew how to do was hand their affairs over to other men. I would never leave them alone at the bakery; I would bark at one of them just because I could, and watch his hands flutter into action, searching for something, anything, to do. I never understood how they could just stand idly by while the fire roared in the oven.

I once nailed a cat as it dashed across the terrace. The shot jolted them out of their chairs. The cat kept running, tripping over its innards before finally keeling over. That shot ripped out Fatima's heart too – she turned her face away, saying nothing, containing her disgust and anger.

'Go and get it off of the terrace', I said.

She went down the four steps towards it, distancing herself and hiding her face from me. There were a lot of them on the *mastaba* and they began to examine my rifle, taking turns lifting it to their shoulders, following the path of an imagined bird, holding it in their sights until they clicked the trigger with the empty casing. They filled the house and Hajja Khadija waited for them to leave so she could put her children's food on the stove. She put her wide skillet near the table's edge, and the oil spattered on the floor and on the walls. The house was cleaner in those days than when we lived on our own and cooked less. I realized that a house doesn't get dirty from being lived in, but rather from things being kept in their places, and from the slowness and lack of movement of only a few inhabitants.

I had stopped peeing on the concrete floor below the *mastaba* before her death as I had built another bathroom on the long and narrow floor space of the kitchen. She had insisted I build one, saying that everyone now had their toilets inside their houses. I put it at the end of the kitchen and built a wall and a door to make it look like it was far from the house and separated from it. But the odors still seeped out to the kitchen and the two rooms beyond it because the narrow little window was not sufficient to carry the smells outside. I told Hajja Khadija that pouring a lot of water would not help since toilets have a smell that emanates even if people don't defecate there – and the smell of an outhouse will stick even when you stop using it.

I went back to urinating on the concrete below the *mastaba* because of my disgust with my own filth drying on the floor of the toilet and the lower parts of its walls. When my son's daughter came down to clean it, she would not step across the threshold; she just poured in a lot of water from the doorway, as she cast her eyes from the storeroom, to the kitchen, to the stairs, up to the attic.

I pee standing on the *mastaba*, with my thighs stuck against the stone railing with the gaps and the carvings. I figured the height of the railing would cover my lower half so they won't see what I am doing, and when I can see that it doesn't really hide me from their vision I just imagine that they are directing their eyes to something else far in the distance. I pee from the *mastaba* night and day, and when I step to the little space at the front, I don't look in the direction of the woman and her children in the upper story of my brother's house, or in the direction of the second woman in the room at the beginning of the *dar*. I step forward without taking note of anything and stick my thighs against the carving of the railing, my back leaning back. They climb the stairwell up to their home on the floor above me, not looking at me standing there staring at them. They appear only briefly, since they shut the door behind them as soon as they arrive and sit there in the darkness while their mother opens up the faucet so that the water doesn't noisily rush out.

I spend my time on my chair, staring at the big gateway of

the *dar*, where I waited for them under the archway after my father died. A man from another village nearby told me not to open fire until they had come through the gate and were completely inside the *dar*. I waited days for them, under the arch – my hand never left my father's revolver. When they appeared at the intersection near the village square my two brothers ran away from the terrace and towards the houses in the flatlands. I waited for them until they gathered in front of the old room. When one of them pushed on the door I let out a loud, high shout. I didn't say anything in particular, it was just a shout. They turned their faces towards me on hearing it and they saw the revolver aimed at them. I was only fourteen. When I went out into the town to walk around after they had left, I felt I had grown years beyond the kids of my generation. When I sat down with my brothers and commanded Mahmoud, who was several years older than me, 'Give me the water, Mahmoud', he got up and brought it over to me. I had caused him to become quiet and humble at home, and he quickly became accustomed to the reversal in status between us. I would see him bowing his head in front of me – he was taller – and I'd ask him, 'Who has hurt you, Mahmoud?' He would turn his eyes, neither questioning nor fearful, towards me. It was like that in public as well. 'Who has hurt you, Mahmoud?' I'd ask and again he would look at me without answering.

Hajj Salim's wife was afraid of me, she and her children too. Whenever they step up to the stairs leading on up to their house they keep their heads bent down and their eyes nailed to the floor. They know I am aware that they are crossing under my entrance, so they step over the threshold in one long stride. I suggested to Hajj Salim that we replace the old doorway with a new one made of iron, but he wouldn't accept that. At the time he had just left his bakery in Beirut and returned to live in the village. He didn't leave for more than a few years, but he came back and fixed up his house as if he'd spent his whole life in Beirut. He put huge sofas in one of the three rooms and locked the door. At the top of the stairs leading to the *mastaba* he installed a low gateway that anyone could cross over just by lifting his feet a little. I said to him: 'Let's get a big tall one for the whole house', but he didn't agree to that. So I paid for it all. But then I began to lock it up at night, and keep the key on me. We tangled a lot over this, and he pounded on the iron door with his hands and feet when he came back from his evening out to find it locked shut. I told him to make an entranceway for his own house and put it in the middle of his terrace. His face took on a mean look and he went up to his house. I stayed in my place and shouted at him as he shut his door behind him. When my voice rang out he pulled open the door again to show me his frowning yellow face, and said words I didn't hear in my headlong rush towards him. I kept wrangling with him until the morning caught up with us, and I heard him move around his house. I got up from my place and pounded on the wall of his *mastaba* with my pickax, swearing at him. He built his gateway one meter into my property.

I only visited him once when he was sick and dying. My children had insisted that I do so. My son Abu Fayez swore that he would never walk in my wake if I didn't. My brother was asleep in his bed and his hands were slim and emaciated, the bones sticking out. His wife, whom he married when he was seventy, said to him, 'Your brother is here, Hajj', and he opened his eyes and looked around for me. He didn't look at any of his children standing around, or at his wife who was busy lifting the blanket to cover his chest and neck. He looked as if he was thinking of something else while he stared at me, not taking his eyes off or letting his head sink back into the pillow until she told him to relax. He turned his eyes away from me towards her, before raising them to the ceiling. They were filling a large portion of his face, which had gone pale and wizened from so much sleeping and illness. Every time he shifted them elsewhere in the room he looked as if he was speaking to something there. Hajj Ali Farhat told me once that a man in his last days regains the features he had the day he was born. That was the same look he had when he stood in front of me with his bluing and swollen eyes, as if he was punishing me for abandoning his friendship, and for acting the way a man of the house acts. He was orphaned at only seven or eight, and I felt sorry for him – more for his frailty and his worn-out oversized clothes than for having been orphaned at a young age.

I bought the gateway with my own money. The iron was painted green, and it had two copper stars at the top that shone in the face of whoever came into the house. I would take my chair and sit under its arch, and see the entire house from where I sat, and I could see the road all the way from the town square to the house entrance.

When Hajj Salim's wife came in with her handful of young

children, I got her to be resourceful in crossing past me so as not to bother me with any noise she might make. She would take care of the endless complications of her and her children's entrance right up to the point that they entered their house. They would close the door and not open it again, and they wouldn't stand on their little balcony overlooking the courtyard of the house. They would keep the two wooden window screens facing my house shut all of the time. I found the woman to be more odd and freakish with every conversation that she had with the neighbor ladies living behind the mosque and alongside it. She forged a link between her house and the neighbors, who despite being close by, were different from us. She would talk to them in a voice I could hear while sitting on the *mastaba* or under the arch of the gateway. And when I got a glimpse of her while passing along the narrow path, she would be stuck to the path's edge as if she hadn't strayed beyond it for a long time.

She turned the back of the house into its front, as if she had just flipped it around, and changed its direction. Hajja Amina, my brother Hajj Salim's first wife, didn't like to stand anywhere other than in the corner of my *mastaba*, below the high wall. The late Fatima almost fell several times trying to climb down from the higher section of the *mastaba* to go to Hajja Zahiya's house. Hajja Khadija told her to take the new path curved off to one side, and she started muttering as if someone had rebuked her or told her that she was a burden upon us, living with us in the house.

Yes, Hajja Amina turned the house around from its original orientation – not in order to speak to her nearby female neighbors, but to make it face her family home – which she could not see, due to the height of the many houses between her and it. I thought she might be taking Hajj Salim's nephews to her family, so I called one of them I saw entering the doorway. He approached me silent and confused, so I asked him about his father and gave him an entire Lebanese pound.

III

I haven't left the house for a year. I spend my time inside, shuffling between the kitchen, the *mastaba*, and the high bed. For more than a year I haven't gone out to the old room, the floor of which I imagine to be covered in dirt from the roof. I haven't gone out to it because there is nothing that I would do there. It was empty, since they moved out all of the last bits of furniture, which they had stacked up against the walls. Even the Qur'anic verse which had covered the little window was no longer in its place. They are waiting for the whole roof to cave in, along with the tree trunks that support it. I told my son Qassem that when it falls it will bring down other rooms with it as it collapses. He didn't say anything. He covered me with a blanket, pulling it up to my chin, and moved the space heater closer. I know they are going to sell the house and leave after I die. He didn't stop the woman next door from building a second story right up against us, bringing her balconies so close that we became totally exposed to her. And he never fixed the window that fell from its rotting frame.

They left the old room empty, a shell. They had moved

out of it several times before, but they used to always leave something that would signal their coming back later on: an old curtain or a bed or a large table that didn't fit in their house. I myself used it as storage space for farm tools after Fatima died. I would go in with my shoes caked in thick mud from the fields and walk around although I knew that Hajja Khadija would not clean up after me. My grandson asked me how we colored the floor that red color, so I asked him back, 'What will you do with it when I die?' He got up from the sofa and headed for the door. They always use my talk of death to wind up a conversation and exit. I remain stretched out on the bed with my head propped up higher than the rest of my body on two big cushions. When they all crowd into their house on the top floor I feel as if my house is flowing out from under me, that I am incapable of holding it together in my mind's eye. I see it as large and variegated, each room pulling the house in a different direction. I stopped opening the pantry room, as there was nothing for me there. And the two little attic spaces of the *tatkheeti* stayed empty as well. I don't remember when we started emptying the shelves. Once I saw Abu Fayez's son leaving the house with the crescent-shaped ax in his hand. I asked him where he was taking it and why he didn't tell me first. He stood there trembling, and lifted it from behind his thigh. 'Take it,' I said to him, 'but don't come back to the *tatkheeti* again.' There are lots of things I could only remember when they were collected and sorted in rows on the shelves.

They all come to the house at the same time. And I never shut any of the doors. There were so many of them that they

39

served to partition the house into a collection of houses. They would flow through the rooms and doorways like the wind, and it got to the point I could no longer tell who was coming and who was going, me sitting there amongst them, my children and whatever visitors they had with them. Hajja Khadija would put her frying pan on the *mastaba* and do her work lazily. I figured her slowness would never feed the large number of human beings who filled the house. She always looked as if she was waiting for a woman to step forward and take the work off of her. They would eat standing, as she finally started serving the eggs. She didn't know how to go about feeding them. I would tell her to bring down the butter pot from the top of the cupboard, but she would hesitate, out of her stinginess.

She didn't learn a thing in my house, but she never forgot a thing either. Her sister Fatima would stand behind the window-pane and watch us eat. She was always hungry. She bought blocks of *halwa* with the money she took from my children. We found her closet filled with it after she died.

The only door of the house that is always open is the door between my room and the *mastaba*. The door of the separate outside toilet has been closed for a long time. I don't open it to look at what might be in there because I know that a thick layer of filthy dust is sticking to the walls and floor, harder to clean than the calcium deposits that stick to the glass of *ibreeqs*. And I no longer enter the cowshed that is a distance from the house. Just one door, a short path from kitchen to bed, and then the *mastaba*. When a man gets to be my age not only do the number of people around him become fewer; the space he moves his body within also shrinks. I went twice to my daughter Nayefa's house at the top of the road. Once, I saw heads from the house's entranceway, but not hers, and so I thought that they were her guests, sitting outside and enjoying the clean village air. They were wearing their pajamas, and when I arrived they rose to greet me. They had me sit down while they were still talking to one another. They even left me behind to go to the other end of the long balcony. And when I rose to leave no one came towards me apart from my daughter Nayefa. She waited for me at the top of the stairs as I was descending them slowly in the faint light. They knew I was leaving because I was furious at them for their being so preoccupied and ignoring me, although that didn't lead them to linger with me. I went back to visit them there one other time. That time I was satisfied just to see the cars slowly passing by under their balcony and the people congregating in the village square. I enjoyed this and was keen not to miss a single person there. I recall stretching my head to see if anyone was standing under the balcony that I hadn't talked to yet.

At home I didn't even hear their loud voices. At their house I distracted myself from the people who were in the house with the people who were outside it. When I got ready to get up and go I couldn't find anyone around me. The house had become vacant, as they had all left except for Nayefa who came out from the kitchen and stood at the top of the stairs. I didn't turn towards her when she spoke to me, and made a show of keeping my attention on where my feet trod on the stairs.

I don't even go into Hajja Khadija's room although I can see everything in there through its open door. And I no longer see Hajj Salim's wall, either. I built this house and know every single stone in it. I even used to go down inside the well and know its flooring and its rounded walls intimately. I recall the men standing around the opening, gripping the knotted rope that was tied around my waist. I was in my seventies and didn't need to look for many reasons to go down there. The last time though, I did get frightened when I was in the pit of the well, so I took to shaking the rope and shouting at them to lift me out of there. My voice echoed back loud and distorted as if coming back at me from every crack in the well. The rounded walls became narrower and narrower the more I was pulled up. I panicked, thinking that the opening might close in on my chest. The water was stagnant and lifeless all around me. When they pulled me out of there my strength had been sapped, and my breathing had become constricted. I sat there at the well's edge panting, trying to catch my breath. I felt a strong urge to fall asleep at their feet, although I was soaking wet and half-naked. I had become tired in my heart, not my body; I was scared. Me, the one who used to tell Hajj Hussein Salih, who was big and strong like an ox, that large bodies had small hearts. I felt I shouldn't spend a long time at the edge of the well, so I got up, weak and dizzy. But I was still able to stand in the middle of them. I was in those white underclothes of mine that went down almost as far as my knees, otherwise I was naked. My body was lean and hard, and there was power still in it, but the strength of a seventy-year-old man really comes from the willpower that is in his heart.

A lean, hard, and strong body – and the years had distributed knobby round lumps and knots throughout my shoulders, forearms, and lower parts of my chest. It was as if my bones were getting more numerous as my body grew older. But I saw strength in this too, just as I used to see strength in my two large and extra-boney feet. I would always take a knife and slice a ribbon of leather off a pair of new shoes, from the place where my bones would protrude, even before I knew whether or not those shoes would hurt my feet.

So I left them standing around the well and headed off to my room. I knew that I would not be successful in keeping my body upright and energetic, or in hiding the curvature that was settling into it. I opted to hurry out to the village square in order to erase my fright and to let them forget what had happened to me. They were gathered together there as if they were waiting for me. I could find no other means of restoring their awe of me than by raising my voice, so I spoke up and told them in a loud voice about what happened to my crops after some cows got into my fields.

They kept silent, casting sideways glances as if hoping to give themselves more time to believe what I was saying. Maybe I should have gone down to the bottom of the well once again to speak to them from the depths. When I walked away from them going back to my house, I realized that they are not the ones I ought to try to frighten, since they would never stand up to me, unless I give them a chance like this to take advantage of me. I got bored there at the well's mouth and started staring at the round walls that widened the further they went down. I let out a loud cry that plunged into it deep and wide, amplified as it spread throughout the dark recesses. Some time passed and I figured the sound had scattered and disappeared on the surface of the water, but it only subsided until it could regroup and come back up to me, just as amplified and as thick as it had been going down. I was someone who goaded his heart into recklessness, a step or two ahead of my natural inclination, so that I could plunge forward heart and soul, head held high and hands flailing, shouting out loud. Not so much to frighten people as to feel my own power in their midst. But it wasn't very long after this happened to me that I sealed the well's mouth with concrete. I sealed the whole opening, but left one small hole for a hose to bring the water up, and another to allow water to fall into it.

Hajja Khadija would distress herself over our little girl Bahija's two boney feet that she'd inherited from me, and ask if the doctors could somehow fix them. When she grew older she started to go overboard, making up her face, and I would look at her and say that it only made her look rougher. Any woman who looks like me is not a beautiful woman. When I first laid eyes on Hajja Khadija, somewhere between our two villages, I didn't soften my voice or avert my eyes. I stood my ground with my feet planted firmly under me and my head held up high. Women do not like beauty in men, but power and force. I heard the neighbor ladies compare me to a cypress tree without any leaves. She didn't say a word in response. She came to me walking barefoot from her village. When I opened the door of my house to her I knew that she had spent a long time waiting in front of it.

My partner in the little bakery that we took over in Ashrafiyah told me we needed to widen the counter, which only accommodated two customers. He thought we could move the high marble counter back a little and narrow it down a bit. He also thought we could put the bakery façade behind our backs and raise it up to extend from the middle of the wall to the edge of the roof. He was undone by his fear of not being able to figure out how to expand the tiny property. So I decided to take over his share and open the bakery from the back wall all the way to the room with the crumbling walls. It wasn't long after I had taken over the whole place before I had expanded – not only to the wrecked room, but up to the little pit behind it. I sold them bread during the day and at night I emptied the place of rubble. I more than doubled the size of the bakery. When I see the workmen's shovels plunging into the earth and flinging it aside, I feel that I am witnessing an explanation for the dreams I used to have about this constricted space that made me and my partner move very little, each of us stuck in our place. In my dream I ask him about the door to the left of the furnace, at times, and about the bathroom wall facing his door, at others; he looks at me astonished, astonished as I am also, and he doesn't dare open it. I do and see that it gives out onto two adjacent and empty rooms. I look back at him and say to him: 'They are mine since I am the one who saw the door and had the courage to open it.'

No sooner than I had expanded that bakery, I abandoned it and took over another in Debbas Square. It was large, so much so that I could never find the workers who were sleeping there. I would shout for them from the middle of the floor and they would appear, sluggish, from under the oven boards and sacks of flour. A wave of sympathy would pass over me whenever I woke them up and saw them looking around, trying to figure out where they were. I knew that in their dreams they were back in the village. If one of them passed in front of the door tired and sleepy, I would shout at him from wherever I was, and his whole body would jolt forward as if a big foot had shoved him from behind. I thought they were going to stay just the way they were; spending their working hours carelessly and unconsciously, and their time off in joking around and laughing. But they changed their habits after they moved on from me.

They partnered with each other in a number of bakeries they acquired in various parts of Beirut. They would change partners with one another frequently, so that one might dump a new partner before the partnership had a chance to gel. No one who saw them in my bakery would think they'd have houses and cars. When I ran into them their faces were pale and emaciated from the amount of work they did. They had the paleness of someone who was drowsy and talking slowly. Whenever I went to the village and mention was made of one or the other of them, I would think they were talking about someone I didn't know. Even Hajj Salim, who was as old as their fathers, left the village when he was fifty years old to work like them. He would dash around his bakery tripping over his workers and customers in his constant movement, holding the loaves in his two hands as if they were going to be in his possession for a long time. When counting the change he would at times ponder and brood, making a mistake, and then drop his hands as if he had, by finishing with one customer and moving on to the next, completed a major piece of work in its entirety. I felt sorry for him because I could see that he was unable to make the movement of his body conform to his age. He seemed not to realize how much time it takes to accumulate wealth, but rather to think that abandoning himself to his work would make him wealthy by the day's end.

He wasn't entirely wrong. In less than a year from his descent to Beirut he had become like them. In those days it only took a year for a newcomer in Beirut to get to the same level as those who had come years earlier. They would straggle in from the village and return home in completely changed circumstances some time later. It seemed to me that piling up a fortune had become easy, something you could do from mere bodily exertion. In those days it had become so easy that one could spend the time required in Beirut without having to change oneself in any way on the inside. As for me, when I sat with them, I would talk to them exactly as I had done before they left for the city. They remained just as they always were, with nothing at all new about them as we sat in the houses they were visiting. They would talk their same talk and the only memories that would come to them were those of their village days.

Hajja Khadija's brother looked as if whatever money he made had been for someone else. Nothing changed in him at all; he would go quiet as soon as they started talking about their jobs. It was as if he had become wealthy in a profession he didn't know. I looked at him sitting there shyly with this sister's same facial expressions. Whenever I saw this face I expected him to get up and go off to the kitchen, as she would do. So I singled him out to try to get him to lift his head up and look me in the eye, and asked him how things were going with him. Not because I missed Hajja Khadija, whom I saw to be fully present in him, but to see how time passes over the dead and departed without those who resemble them resembling them any less. I told him to stay to have lunch together, but he is timid and doesn't know how to reply. He goes out with them, without turning towards me, so that I don't repeat my invitation and further embarrass him.

That's also how he was when he came to visit us before she died. He stood at a distance from her and gazed out at the plants in the basin below the railing and didn't speak. He spent a long time standing there without moving, with her just a few steps away. Their sister Fatima appeared like a stranger, separated from them by her appearance, which is not at all like theirs. She stayed in the old room, busying herself as if he had only come to visit her sister. And he forgot to take his leave of her when he left, but then came back into the middle of the house to announce that he had forgotten to say goodbye to Fatima. She was many years older than the two of them, and that made me think that she was not part of the family history I knew. It was as if she had come to them from an earlier life, lived before joining them.

I would push her with my hands to the terrace and to the cow shed, and shout at her whenever I saw her standing hunchbacked in the middle of the house. I think she didn't understand my scolding and shouting, because she would go right back to standing just as she was the minute my voice died out. Before

I started standing near her bed I didn't know that her hatred for me would bring her to forget herself completely. Hajja Khadija knew this, but didn't say anything about it, as if it were a woman's secret, one that they hold within themselves all of their lives. She wasn't surprised at Fatima's intolerance towards me, and she would appear, when talking to her, as if she were addressing a rational, sane woman, somewhere down inside her. She told me not to scold her and make her angry, not to 'give her attributes I don't see are in her'. How could someone who stands like that, absent-minded and distracted, in my way and not budging until I push her with my hands, even *get* angry? I don't get to know people since I always go by their appearances.

I don't understand how Abu Hisham could wait for his brothers to come, for them all to go and visit their mother, under whose window children gathered to hear her talking to herself, gesticulating with her hands in unfathomable ways. They would always go to her together, even waiting in the street for anyone who was late and had to catch up with them, so that they could go in as a group. Whenever I passed by her window on the street and heard her talking all alone in the darkness of her room, with its low-lying ceiling, I became more convinced that she didn't recognize anyone. I'd ask her: 'How's your health, Afifa?' She wouldn't answer or look at me. She'd go on with her jabbering, moving her hands as if she was measuring something that wouldn't stand still.

I think to myself how old age is hard on women, how quickly their bodies change and waste away, how their lips narrow and tighten, and their eyes fade. As if they acquire, early on, the

49

shared and always similar features of their old age. Then a long period of decay settles into them, as if their souls are slowly and gradually coming out over all the years they have left. Hajja Khadija's tall body rescued her from this fate of early senility, and her movements and features did not age prematurely. But she gave up on intercourse and came to detest it. She would bring the youngest son to bed with her once he had fallen asleep, and then would sneak off to sleep herself. I would say to her that growing up sleeping in his mother's bed will spoil him. I started leaving her in Beirut when I would come to the village for a number of days. When I'd get back I'd find the house in chaos from all the visitors and family.

My daughter Bahija was preoccupied with painting her face and plucking her eyebrows, as if she was just about to leave the house; her sister, who has been stricken by a disease that thinned out her hair, spent all her time working in the house. The wives of my two elder sons were also there, along with their relatives who would come visiting and stay on, with Hajja Khadija hanging about as if she was one of them. She would be all but lost in their midst, so that I used to think that some other woman must be distributing all of the household chores to everyone, and assigning Hajja Khadija her share. I'd see her strolling through the house with the kerchief on her head, suggesting she was soaking wet with her preoccupation with the laundry and floor mopping. The chaos increased to the point that they were not able to hide their toiling from me when I was among them. Bahija would bring me my food, so I would question her about the loud voices I heard as I climbed the stairs. She always stood in front of me in her full beauty, and I know by her smile, a smile that she can put on her face whenever she wants, that she is the strongest of the lot. I handed over the management of the house to her, and gave her money to cover the expenses. Who taught her to stand like that, like a man, when she comes to visit me in my house? She doesn't linger very long, just the time it takes to remove the food she has prepared from the bags. She shows it to me before placing it in the pantry. She withdraws after that, just as she did when she was a little girl, lots of make-up filling her strong smiling face.

She doesn't linger long at my home. She keeps her kids waiting in the long passage between the gateway of the compound and my house. One of them leaning on the opened door of the car and the other crying out for her from time to time in a voice that he thinks is loud enough for her, but not for me, to hear. Maybe a third will come over and stand under the window and wave with his hand to her from behind the glass. None of their boys or girls visits anymore. Qassem's son, who I used to take with me to Nabatiyah, passes quickly under my window or by my door on his way to the stairs. His father himself comes down to make me tea when the house fills with women, his daughters and daughters-in-law. When I see him bent over sweeping my floor I get the feeling that they have expelled both of us, and that he must have sat there quietly a long time before getting up, to come down to me. He comes closer to me to sweep under my bed, and I ask him about his health, since he is contorting his body in a way that is not in keeping with his age. But he doesn't speak to me unless it is to ask about what I am eating. So I will keep quiet until he is done and he stands by the door about to go upstairs again; that's when I will tell him something to try to keep him down with me a little longer.

They only stay a little while. Whoever sees them going and coming must think I spend my whole day with them. They see the time moving along heavily when they are with me. When their feet step beyond the threshold their movements become slower. And their time flows by slow and easy. The time Bahija spends talking to them while they are up on their balcony is many times greater than the time she spends visiting me. I still hear her voice talking to them when I awake, after having fallen asleep listening to her, back when she had just started talking to them. Then her children will stop urging her to hurry up; the one hanging on the car door takes a few steps towards the compound and greets everyone, standing not far from his mother.

I don't go out of my room to the *mastaba* until they have left the compound and I am alone. When I see that it is empty, I sit down in my chair and begin to brood in the quiet that they left behind them. By then it will be the very end of twilight, so I can no longer make out the shape of the gateway. Their noise becomes fainter as it dissipates. I rest my entire arm on the stone railing and decide to remain there a long time, sitting in my chair. Slowly but surely I can no longer hear a sound from them upstairs, and can no longer make out the edges of the four steps leading from my house to the compound yard. I don't fall asleep in my chair. I say to myself: after a while they are going to come back out on their balconies from their rooms, and the uproar is going to start all over again.

IV

It's like I'm reliving the memories of other men. Or as if that was some other boy cursing and casting stones at the shepherds who'd let their cows stray too close to my father's land. Or maybe I was just a passer-by, or someone sitting inside, when this person – me, in fact – stepped on the polished white marble tiles at the entrance of the bakery. Sometimes I think back and recall the scene of them standing there and talking behind the door left opened onto the little terraces belonging to my uncle Sheikh Mahmoud, the ones with the very narrow sections. But I don't know if that was something that was said to me or if I saw it with my own eyes. I can envisage them talking, but without the sound of their voices. And all I can picture of them is their heads and their chests stuck to one another as they surge forward trying to reach a man, maybe Uncle Sheikh Mahmoud himself.

What I was told about these events counts as much as what I saw of them, given my distance from their actual occurrence, something now in the distant past. When I see myself as a boy stoning the other boys, I simultaneously see myself remembering the scene at a later stage of my life. As if

I am remembering my remembrance of the same things. The memories come to me clouded, as if covered in white dust. And they come intermittently as well, since there are now paths covering the distances that separate me from them. They are like scattered patches over a vast surface. When I go towards them in my remembrances, I feel I am in an ancient and strange land, and so give up and get out of my bed or my chair near the railings of the *mastaba*. I busy myself with thinking about what hasn't yet become a memory. Maybe with the things my son Qassem said to me before taking his leave, or with the noise of the children who played in the *dar* before scattering off to their homes.

The two men from the clan of the *muezzin* who sat by the side of the road, emaciated and hungry, they too seem like something I was told about. Their appearance was rendered even more bizarre by their eyes, themselves widened by the weakness in their dull-witted and contorted faces. They looked at me in unison, waving their hands. I become frightened. That was something related to me, or else it was something I saw in one of my old dreams. I get out of bed, pushing the covers away with one quick movement, as if brushing away a little animal that has suddenly jumped onto my chest.

I know, when my feet touch the ground, that I am still asleep because the image of the two starving men returns to me. I stretch my hand out to grab my cane. I see my chair propped against the railing, and know then that my son Qassem has swept the *mastaba* before going up. They are sitting on the balcony above me; their voices, which are not particularly raised, nonetheless reach me. I hear no children among them. They drive them out of the *dar* to have the house to themselves. They sit there with the coffee that my son's wife boiled up in order to stretch out the time and increase the amount of talk.

There is also coffee on my daughter Nayefa's balcony. They sit there in their pajamas, quietly, as if the noise from the square down below doesn't reach them. I don't know when they will take off and return to Beirut, because they don't say goodbye to me and their faces don't change at all when they see me, so I can't tell if they have just arrived or if they are still hanging on after a long visit. I left my Beirut house for them to move into. Whenever they want something from me they come to me with all of their children, as if to demonstrate to one another their intentions. My daughter's husband pulled the power of attorney waiver and the ink pad out of his pocket, so I knew they were intent on concluding the business in one sitting. I gave them my thumbprint. Afterwards, they sat mumbling in their chairs for a while. But my daughter's husband practically left for his house right away, as he was folding the power of attorney waiver and putting it back in his pocket. My daughter Nayefa brought a bowl of water to wash the ink off of my thumb. The house in Beirut was high up, and the last time I climbed up the stairs I had to sit down in exhaustion on the stairs, with two floors still to go. When Nayefa came down to help me climb up the rest of the way, I remembered how my two boys would race down the five floors to carry their sister, sick with her heart condition, upstairs. They would carry her sitting on a chair, her thick hair practically deadening her face before its time. They made her a bed in the big room opening on to the balcony, to pass the long periods of exhaustion. They would say to her: 'Sleep, so that you get better.' She would look at them with her eyes that were becoming larger and wider with each passing day.

Nayefa would stay at home by herself during the day because her children and husband only came back at sunset, when their work wound up. The material on the sofas in the sitting room where I would spend my time was the same material that she made her clothes with. She made the house look like her, after she had expelled all of my other children from it. The skinny legs of the sofa, seen from below, even looked like her bony legs. I spent my day by myself in boredom because she didn't leave her kitchen to come be with me. I call her, and when she comes I tell her to look on the radio for certain stations. She set about shaking it with her two hands as if forcing it to work in spite of itself, and then quickly returned to the kitchen. I tell her to give it back to me once she has exhausted her patience with it. I'd pick it up and it would start hissing and spurting and screeching distorted and unintelligible sounds, and then I'd turn it off and place it by my side. I ate very little when she came in with a steaming tray, and she was peeved that I didn't eat enough to be grateful or to express any thankfulness to her. But she forced herself to act amiably and tried to get me to eat, forcing herself to say, 'Come on and eat, daddy'. I'd pull the blanket up to cover my upper body, and turn away. I spent my time listless and bored in Beirut. Except for two instances – when I would peer into other people's balconies, and the moment I climb out of the car – I don't like the building.

When I was living there I used to climb the five flights of stairs holding my chest up and my head high, not once steadying myself with my hand on the stairwell railing, and never stopping to rest. There were lots of inhabitants there, so many that I used to meet them going up or coming down and think that they were either on their way up some place further above me, or else were done doing whatever they had come to do. At the level of the broad window between the third and the fourth floor, two women always stood in the stairwell; whenever they saw me coming they'd turn towards me and want to have some fun, but I'd check them with a scornful look and keep climbing up. I figured back then that my boys, who hadn't been married that long, were still too young for these Beirut women who, the minute they set foot into the bakery, headed straight my way.

I'd continue my ascent home, to the house where the door was always open. There were lots of people in the house. I remember them, but can't picture Hajja Khadija amongst them. That's because I get things mixed up with the summer she spent by herself in the village. My mind will stretch out her months there to cover over half of my entire stay in Beirut.

I tell them to take me back to the village, and they say wait another two days until the weekend when they have some time off. I tell them 'Take me back', knowing I am going to hand the house over to them, since I don't feel comfortable living there. I stamped my thumbprint on the paper which was the purpose for which they all came, because I could see that there was nothing left in it for me. I had decided that anyway, before they even came, yet I was peeved at seeing my daughter's husband greedily holding the paper in his hands, carefully folding it, so pleased with himself, his shifty eyes betraying his contempt for us. I stopped looking at him because I knew exactly how my face would look to him behind my thick glasses. I can't steal a glance at someone any more, the way they can – I have to look at a thing with my whole head, and with my body as well. It must look as if I am oblivious to everything when I am busy peering at something, and seem that I can't hear what is going on around me. He moved all of the sons I had with me right out of the house. Not through the strength of his character, but more with his creepy silence and shifty eyes. Or with his evident self-satisfaction whenever he managed to do something, like someone counting some cash he just acquired from people sitting there. His father Hajj Salim and I could never stop fighting over the wall he constructed a meter on to my land.

Once I banged on that wall with my pickax making to demolish it, but he just sat there in his house sneering at me, but afraid of me at the same time. Despite all this, I bequeathed my house to his son, my daughter's husband, after he had managed to get rid of my sons, one after the other. I stamped my thumb on his paper, and right then and there he started to look like his father, with his distracted eyes and his fidgety way of sitting. In both of my visits to his house in the village, he left me sitting in the chair, and went to the far end of the balcony with his brother and brother-in-law. Now I made no mistake in not bestowing any land on my daughters. That would have meant nothing more than giving my property to their husbands, and their children after them.

Sayyid Mahdi told me that what I did was not something God recommended and that it is something I should have refrained from doing, but I took my three sons and walked them over every piece of my properties, scattered all over the village and its surroundings. I left the girls nothing but the little terrace by the threshing floor – and they kept wrangling over that, right up until my eldest daughter died. Now I know I was not wrong to do what I did – having lived all these many years. The girls' kids are nice and close to us when they are little, but the older they get the more they go off and turn against us. They move away from us.

Bahija's kids stay outside when their mom comes to visit me. When I look at them they look skinny with long narrow heads, just like their uncles and all of their father's family's children. I didn't will them any land. Just the threshing-floor terrace which they went and fought over, even though what it was worth wouldn't have covered the court costs if they decided to take it to the court. When Sayyid Mahdi told me: 'Give them some land too', I kept the bit he had in mind for myself. I told him I was keeping it for my future. He laughed. I guess he figured I was talking like someone much younger than I was. Hajja Khadija was still alive; although she was weakening and losing her strength, though she'd been diagnosed with no illness. Sayyid Mahdi laughed again when he came to understand that I was getting ready for something the way young men get ready for things. Hajja Khadija would spend her time sleeping on her bed, and whenever she got up she would spend some time dizzily stumbling along to the toilet. I thought she was going to die, so I started going to

Marwaniyah all dressed up and clean-shaven, visiting people I knew a long time ago. The woman they took me to see was a widow, not much older than forty. I sat there in my suit and *tarboosh* with my shaved head and face, and must have appeared taller than all of them. They were all busy talking, their backs hunched over as if to make me stand out from among them. She was elegant and lithesome, but she didn't seem to know if she was meant to remain silent or to move about and walk among us. She didn't know what to do. When we took our leave, the people with me said that she was upset and that this was not like her. So I came to her alone on the second visit. I stood for a while at the door holding the bag that I had filled with soaps and perfumes and stockings like the women in Beirut wear. Her house seemed more confined and constricting than on the previous visit. When I entered I did not stutter or stammer, and I headed right for where I had sat the last time. In her house clothes, which she straightened out in a hurry, she appeared younger. I had forgotten how to speak with women, and I tried not to act the way I do in front of my sons' wives. I changed my voice and my demeanor, to rid my face of the features I adapt when I am with men. She started asking me if I had tired on the way, and if I was hungry. She offered to make me something to eat.

I didn't stay very long in her house, which I never visited again. As she was seeing me off, she spoke easily and slowly, taking her time, and she seemed intent on standing silently, right next to me. Saddled up next to her, I saw that she was short, and I felt pleased at my height.

This was to be the first time my sons ever raised their voices to my face. I knew Qassem had worked out his speech along the way from Beirut, and that he had struggled to keep quiet the whole time on the road, persuading himself not to show his anger and lose his cool. The three of them stood there, knowing that if they sat down I would be able to deflect them from what they had come to do. They started in with just a few words, but with determination. And then they finished off what they had wanted to say standing over Hajja Khadija, lying there in her bed. When they left the room they couldn't face me and didn't turn my way. Their faces were stormy and furious as they went down the four steps to the courtyard in front of the *dar*. From the window, their big bodies appeared to be drooping and exhausted from work, from sitting around in houses. I felt ashamed of myself because of Hajja Khadija, and didn't go to her room. But I didn't leave the house either. I started to pace between my room and the kitchen, where I started making noises, banging pots and pans onto the table. When I heard her voice calling I went out to meet her. I sat her on a chair that was half-way between her room and the kitchen. She was panting, and her graying head was twisting and turning, right and left, as if she were complaining of her constant pain. She didn't say anything, as if she had only come out to see for herself what all the commotion was about. She wasn't angry, just in pain. When I put her back into bed she began to shiver, so I covered her and sat next to her until she slept.

I gave her the piece of land that their ownership had managed to destroy. They let her trees dry up, and allowed her footpaths to get clogged up with thistles and high brush.

Whenever I think about that land, I find that it seems to have split off from our village and attached itself to other nearby villages. No matter how different those plots might have been one from the other, they all looked the same to me. I could distinguish them from the terraces that surrounded them, standing on the roof of my house. And I could make out the precise line that divided my share from my brother Mahmoud's share, even from that distance.

Once I passed the age of seventy I sped up the process of handing over my lands to them. I would wait for them to come to the village, and I'd spend the entire time with them, while they stood around morosely waiting for the food to be prepared so they could busy themselves with eating. They became even more sullen after I had distributed the land to them. They would hold onto their little children while lounging about, with one or the other of them getting up every once in a while to talk to his wife – as if it wasn't going to be possible for him to spend the entire night with her in bed. And they never once would tell Hajja Khadija not to stand so close to the big frying pan that was always on the verge of burning her, since she didn't know how to move it around. She would spend the whole time staring at it, and when they would leave she stood for them at the edge of the *mastaba*, her two arms clutching her belly. She would say her goodbyes before even having had a chance to talk to them. I figured that was because they all came together at once, so one time I pulled one of them aside after his brothers had all gone out, and told him to wait a little while until the sun cooled down. He waited, but only right there by the edge of the *mastaba*, never taking his eyes off the high gateway or the cars that were speeding down from the other end of the road.

I also gave the house I'm living in to them. As I've said before, my son Qassem will sell it when I die. He compares it with the houses that they built at the edge of the village. All he sees is an ancient rambling house with rooms spread all over the place and a roof shedding dirt and pebbles onto the floor below. And he figures that the cow dung stuck to the floor of the cow shed is going to prevent him from sprucing it up and making some use of it. My youngest son didn't spend any time with the land I passed on to him. When people talk to him about it when he comes up from Beirut he starts to joke, to have me understand that it isn't even worth talking about, in terms of its value. He never goes to look at it. I think that maybe he got less land than his two brothers, and nearly promise him the last piece I have, the one I kept for myself. But whenever any one of them comes to visit two times without much of an interval between each visit, I think, 'I must have done that one wrong'. My youngest son will come to me alone, without his family, and will sit in front of me a long time without talking. He gets me water when I ask for it, and he grabs me with both of his hands whenever I want to get out of my bed. I find that I feel close to him when we are alone, and I'll start to talk to him like I did when he was little. So I gave him the piece of land that I had kept for myself.

Even my two daughters become dearer and closer to me when they visit more often. Bahija gives me my food and fixes up the room all around me. So I start to talk to her about her sister – just as I talk to her sister about *her*, when her kids are waiting impatiently for her to finish and leave.

It doesn't take me long to be content. I regretted what I said about my Nayefa, because I thought she wouldn't come back to visit me again. I said a lot of things about her in front of the whole lot of them, and didn't know how to stop myself. And my deciding to withdraw to my room didn't help anything, since I would return to them after going a certain distance in her direction. I'd remember something as I walked away, and my rage would well up and I'd explode at them. My cane would shake and I'd tremble from the loudness of my voice. They'd listen to me for a while and then busy themselves with talking, after one of them nodded to the others. One time in particular, I stand there for some time, while they talk, still full of fury, before I finally turn to leave. The woman who is in the apartment on the top floor of my brother's house stands silently on her balcony; she has stepped out to hear us argue. But then she glances away and leans in some other direction when I look up at her. She is quicker than me because I have to stand firm in my place and raise my entire head towards her in order to see. I cursed my daughter Nayefa one more time because of that woman and hurried off again, shakily, to the four steps – which I took at a fast pace.

The women lingered about clustered with their menfolk, in the narrow spaces left around their cars. I know they are going back and forth, talking about me, over the car roofs. For they waited for me to go back inside before they would all talk together again as a group. I just sat down on my chair, with the cigarette that I had lit trembling in my hand.

Their men let them do the talking and then stand around half-listening, in boredom, looking as if they are waiting for someone to come down from the upper floors of the houses. I don't start to regret what I did until I get out of the chair with the commotion that was filling my head beginning to die down. It thins out slowly before it finally comes to an end and I get up and go to the sink. I say to Nayefa, when she comes, to take the 10,000 pounds that I had on the top shelf of my tall closet, and keep the money in her possession. She takes it. Although she knows that I won't leave it with her for very long. Pretty soon I will pass the money over to someone else that I have become happy with. Qassem asks me: 'Who has that 10,000 pounds?' I think for a while before answering. He tells me I should go buy food with it. I reply that I was just keeping it for my carcass, so he gets angry, although he knows that I talk like that just to say that no one visits me and that I am alone. He refrains from telling me that I won't be alive to buy food for the mourners or, at the end of the day, to pay for the recitation of the Qur'an.

I shift the 10,000 pounds amongst them and forget whom I left it with last. I almost ask Nayefa about it before remembering that it was with her sister. She brought the money to me one day after I had started wondering where it was. She put it in my hand, as I was sitting in bed, to let me know that she was doing me a favor by keeping it for me. I don't know what to do with her when she is with me. I gave them the house I am living in because I no longer know what to do with what I own. Whoever owns something needs to be able to leave his house on his own, but I have to wait days for one of them to come and take me to get my hair cut or to get a shave. They'll ask me why I am letting my hair grow out like that. I just keep silent without answering. They don't come back to ask the question again, because they know that if they do, my angry refusal to talk will come to an end. I run my hand through my beard and find that it is soft and long. I play with it, distracting myself. But I will stand waiting for them near their cars to raise my voice if any one of them asks why I am standing there.

V

I can see the woman who lives in the top story of my brother Hajj Salim's house, but I don't see my son's wife. Those two women talk together for hours in low voices that no one but them can hear, despite the length of the old room separating them. But I know full well they are talking about me, because the woman looks in my direction and gestures towards me, sometimes smiling, as if agreeing with something my son's wife has said. When I lower my head I can feel the two of them up there above me, and I sense that here below I am at an equal distance from both of them. There is no one else besides us three in the *dar*. Their husbands left, together with the woman's children, bowing their heads as they passed through the gateway.

If I stomp on the ground with my foot to shake away the flies, the woman says: 'He is stomping on the floor'. The flies hover about a while and then congregate once again between my toes. I slip my feet back a little so that the spots the flies are heading for are removed safely under the leather of my slipper. My son's wife usually sits in front of the opened door to the roof of the old room. She knows how I am sitting and what I am doing. I lift my head and sit back a bit, as if I am getting ready to take a nap on the chair. I think maybe they will shut up and forget about me; stretching out and shutting my eyes should divert the course of their conversation, and maybe push the woman to go back inside her house.

But I see that she is still in her place when I straighten up after a short while. She must think I can't make her out with my glasses slipping so far away from my eyes. I do have to spend some time gazing at her location before I can actually see her. I try to gather together her shaking, cloudy form to consolidate a picture that – when I am able to hold it – transforms her. She turns her head in the other direction, as if thinking of something that might solidify by looking at the road. My son's wife knows that I look at the women, so she begins adjusting the clothes that are wrapped about her. She pulls them up from between her short, flexed thighs.

She no longer comes down to my house. Once my cousin Hajj Youssef came to my bakery in Beirut and told me that she had taken the children and gone back to her family in Nabatiyah. Qassem, who was no more than twenty at the time, was her husband. When he came to the bakery I told him to send 3,000 pounds to her to entice her to return. Cousin Hajj Ahmad jumped up from his place in the chair and said angrily that women were not cows to be treated in that way. I hadn't wanted to upset him, because the poor man had to spend his days in Beirut with nothing to do. This guy didn't know how to behave when he came to the bakery, because he thought that the money I made has changed me. So I let his remark go, and even said something nice and friendly to him, to sweeten him up. He stood there in the *franji* clothing he hadn't yet gotten used to. Qassem stood between us, at a loss, and I could tell from his silent, stupefied face that he was agitated by his lust for her. How quickly men get all hot and bothered for women who've left them.

A few days later he would come and stand close by me, expecting me to tell him to go to Nabatiyah and track her down. He didn't do anything but stand there, didn't even say he missed his two sons. His face looked strange to me, and I try without success to guess at what's eating him. He seemed unfamiliar, and even his lust was something he must have cultivated in other people's homes. When her brother came to me I knew for certain that I hadn't been mistaken in my view of her. As he was speaking I just watched him work his big dumb mouth, not hearing what he was saying.

She doesn't come down to my house anymore. I used to tell myself, once all of her children had grown up, that I ought not to shout in her face, but later I would carelessly forget this. I take three or four steps towards her, as if I am about to slap her; she lifts up her head and hardens her frame, challenging me to do it. I swing myself away towards the stairs, and can't control the words spouting from my mouth. I tell my Qassem that she is the best of all of my sons' wives, and that she looked after me in my life, while he shifts about distracting himself from what I am saying. He knows I will change my tune after a while, just as I do when speaking of my two daughters whenever I am pleased with one of them. I'll be hard on the other one for a short time, until the two switch places, and I stop favoring the first.

I relax and sink down into the chair, let go of my body and let my head nod downwards so that I'll appear asleep. I know she is describing me to my son's wife and that she is enjoying herself while she is at it. She likes just thinking that she is causing me to imagine that she is talking about me. I place one of my legs over the other, thinking that I will hide both of them and not appear long and thin stretched out in front of my upper body which has become shorter with my stooped back and emaciated belly. Those extra bones in my feet keep my legs long and strong. Looking at them, I see they haven't changed all that much. I keep them uncovered and walk out onto the *mastaba*, in clothes that don't come down to my knees. I figure they won't go slack and limp if I keep them uncovered like that. The body doesn't become old and infirm until it gets used to being covered up in clothes and starts needing more of them all the time. I wear two or three shirts under the pajama top, all of the buttons of which I do up. I stretch my two legs forward and see that they are still strong from those extra bones in my feet and from my walking the long distances between the house and the far-off pieces of land that I kept for myself. I used to arrive with both of them tired out and shaking, but I knew that I was storing up strength for the years to come, by working them like that. I stretch them out in front of me in the sun and I feel them with my hand and find they are hard and muscular, ending thick in my huge feet. A few days after coming to the house I went around barefoot, intentionally showing them to Hajja Khadija so that she wouldn't think we were going to end our lives in the way she envisaged, which after all was what brought her to me. She didn't know, in those days, how she had to behave, so she would stumble around not sure what kind of expression she should wear. I would leave her alone in the house and go out. When I got back I would be careful to keep my expression strangely distant. I would shake off my slippers, which had taken on the shape of my feet, in front of her, and she would take them and put them away where they were supposed to go, as if she were doing just another one of her little chores.

Those two women spend their time whispering about me. Sometimes when the woman finds something new to relate, she will head quickly over to my son's wife, stepping over the low wall which runs between the two of them. In her rush her feet pound the ground with all the weight of her thighs and buttocks. So I tell my son Qassem, when he comes by, that it's her who is making the earthworks fall from the roof of the old room. He says I only say that because I hate her. Otherwise, he'll ask why bits of the roof don't come down when his whole family is staying up late and chatting on the roof. He tells me that I need to cut out talking about whoever is in the house, as their business is none of mine. When he climbs back up to his house I see the woman reply to his greeting, first smiling and then laughing, and I'll know he made some joke about her husband's sleeping in the daytime. He jokes with her so as not to appear angry in the remarks that the two exchange, his wife and the woman, and also to please his wife and make her laugh. And his wife knows that when she is tidying up and cleaning the house, she is at the same time cleaning and taming his moods. She puts out his food the minute he gets home, like a bribe to keep him quiet. She'll brew coffee for the two of them to drink, as well. They use coffee to get their menfolk to leave work early, and they use it to prepare the men to listen to what they have to say, to keep them sitting down, slow-moving and soft-spoken. She will come with the coffee pot and cups, for her sons and their wives, so they can prolong their sitting around in chairs and enjoy what they have to say. Their voices come to me faintly and quietly, so I can't catch any of it, although I am sitting right under them. I hear only high screeches and hubbub. Hajja Khadija never thought to have them all sit together when they were standing scattered over the *mastaba* waiting for her cooking. Their being so restless and scattered apart only made her awkwardness with the frying pan that much worse. But when we were alone in the house, she brought the dinner in too soon. One plate, full of whatever she has cooked, and I will have to ask her: 'Where is the onion, Khadija?' She just didn't know how to feed people. When I finish eating I have to shout out to her in her room to bring me some water. Sayyid Mahdi remarked to me one time that he never saw me outside of the house in her company. I concurred with him without having to even appear to reflect on the issue, since it had occurred to me previously that I had no idea what she might look like walking down the street. 'Neither outside nor inside, Sayyid Mahdi', I said, implying I didn't get close to her in bed either.

I said that not only to Sayyid Mahdi, but to many other people as well. I heard Ali Hashem telling my sons that I have been sleeping alone for more than twenty years. His face had taken on an air of seriousness, as if he was in the process of trying to convince them of something. But they just started laughing and joking around about 'his backside' and 'his thing'. This kind of talk amuses them when it relates to me, because they think I fantasize about having any libido, and that men who have gone beyond the age of seventy can relieve their feeble desires just by talking. When I told them I sleep alone I wasn't thinking about any woman, and had no intention of remarrying. I was simply telling them, perhaps to prepare them for an eventuality that can suddenly come to pass. I didn't like my brother Hajj Salim's second wife, despite her cleanliness and her soft-spoken way – there was something servile about her.

In the mornings, after her marriage, the sound of her sliding open the iron bolt on their bedroom door would ring out before she came out of the room, to give the impression that the night passed for the two of them the same way it passes for young newlyweds. I tried to imagine him stretched out and yawning on his bed, and then strutting about, but the picture would get mixed up with the way I knew he looked at his age, and it blurred with images I had of him from different stages of his life. And then loud clattering would come from her kitchen crockery as she got breakfast ready for him. I didn't like her. I told myself that Hajja Khadija wasn't going to live to see me at an age in which I would feel embarrassed talking about marriage. When he comes out to his *mastaba* in his pajamas I think that it is me who should have gotten remarried, because it's my heart that's still unruly and grumpy.

It isn't an actual woman, but rather fleeting images of clothing and laughs and ways of talking and various foods that I gather from various women whom I find resemble one another. I used to take my chair to the little courtyard between the road and the entrance to the *dar*, and sit there with the ladies while they joined their husbands around sunset. They would delay their return to their houses and spend a lengthy time conversing as they stood on the *mastabas* and low-lying steps. I confuse and mix them up in my mind, shifting my vision from one to the other. I become disoriented and confused, and realize that what I really yearn for is their young age, the cleanliness of their bodies, and their clothes, which give them a glow that will fade as life takes them onwards. They know that I am staring at various parts of their bodies, so they adhere to the edge of the *mastabas* and the walls, crowding up against them. My brother Hajj Salim spent six months traipsing around the villages in search of a woman. When he brought one back I could see that he hadn't given much consideration to her shape, but perhaps more to her clothing, which was very like the clothing his son's wives wore. She is pretty from behind (as I almost said to him when he asked me). It wasn't long though before she became just like all the other women of the villages. They ought to live in Beirut and not come to the village for more than a few weeks a year. I move my eyes among them. When they are all crowding into the *dar*, if there are any unfamiliar women around I don't go back to my room, but stay standing there, agitated by their numbers and the crowd.

I stretch out my legs so that that woman sees that they are

much longer than half the length of my body. It's as if I grew old from above, while my legs stayed in their sixties. I told Qassem that she is stamping around too much on the roof. He can't seem to imagine the plumpness of her rear or the loud bumps she produces which sound like large branches banging against the dried-mud roof. I hear the thumping from the middle of the roof when I see her running to my son's wife. I don't only think of her hard and inflexible buttocks but of her whole heavy backside which convulses whenever she drops one of her feet to the ground. As Qassem says, I hate her. But I hate both of them, that woman and my son's wife, whom I can never quite find the words to describe. So I curse her and say nasty things about her homely and imbecilic family in Nabatiyah. I say things like that to her while having in my mind something else, like for instance the color of her dull-witted face, her large teeth, her slack, open mouth, and her constant hateful, inquisitional stare – all of these things at once.

In women we don't really see much variety, in terms of attributes or characteristics, as we do in men. With women, we either like them or despise them, and that's that. We never say, as we might when describing a man, that she is different from what her looks suggest. Women are just the way they look, the way their shapes are. They can't be any different from what we see in them. I think that their beauty and goodness, or else their ugliness and nastiness, is what goes into their heads and thinking. My son's wife will stand up to deflect my insults and I see that her words come right out of her face, just the way her stares and glances do when she is looking at something. Nothing changes at all when she is moving from a silent mode to a talking mode. She talks as if her face is working to round out and put the finishing touches to its own dumb, clueless imbecility. I shake my cane and raise it in front of her, and she will raise up her head, lower her hands, and open her eyes as widely as she can, challenging and daring me. She knows I shake my cane and raise my hands but don't strike, as if I only do so as a substitution for raising my voice to its loudest level; after that I'll go downstairs cursing and swearing. Qassem doesn't say anything when he comes, and I know he decided to keep quiet about it the minute he comes into the room. He puts the plate of food in front of me and pours me some tea in the glass that he hasn't washed sufficiently. 'Come and have a bite with me, son', I say, but he just mutters a word or two and gathers himself to go back upstairs. I know he will have forgotten everything in the morning, because he is like me and can't stand to maintain a demeanor of animosity for very long.

He puts the plate of food on my table, frowning, his eyebrows furled, causing me to think that I must have done him wrong in some way, or that he did something wrong to me. Scowling like that, he seems to want something he doesn't dare ask for. He appears to me in a way that he only has done one time previously: tall, pale-skinned, large, and full-bodied, and with big eyes – but without having reached full manhood. On that previous occasion he passed in front of me as he was coming into the bakery and I saw paleness about him like the paleness little toddlers have between their legs when they are taking their first steps, and stumbling. Tall and big-framed, but looking like he was raised on nothing but milk, not a hair on his body and no odor whatsoever. It was just one instant, but it was to me a milestone that separated two phases of his life, and the impression it made on me was strong. I can summon up that image of him whenever I want to feel sorry for him or act kindly towards him. He stood face-to-face in front of me, silently, after he had put down the tea glass. He seemed to me to be upset or angry, and confused about what to do with his anger. So I said to him, as I did on this present occasion, 'Come and have a bite with me, son'. He knew by that I was trying to restore the relationship between us, but he coughed nervously and cleared his throat because his confusion had only gotten worse. It was like I had caught him in one of those traps that are easy to wriggle out of. I told him to leave right away, so he left. I felt happy knowing that what had transpired between us was not something that he could tell his wife.

He was a big, tall child, fragile on the inside, as if his innards were contained only by his skin, and not by any meat and bone. There were times when I would see myself in him. This aspect of life jumped right out at me as I was sitting there on my chair. *Then* I realized that I knew the demeanor from long before that specific moment with Qassem passing by me at the bakery. Apart from the photograph I had taken of myself at forty, I really don't recall my having any other comportment in life than this one. I remember the extra bones in my feet, my fingers, certain movements of my body, and some bits of my face in the mirror. But I can't bring this body of mine back to the time when it was young and solid. So then: in order to get the women to drop their chatter and giggling in the *dar*, I get them to stand up straight in their bodies, in front of me, with me simultaneously standing in front of them, but in a body that I can cover up and reveal at will. Not for their sake, but for mine. Otherwise, how could I ever imagine the body of a woman with any longing, if my own body were not standing just as hard and as young opposite one?

When I went to see the woman in Marwaniyah I didn't know how to talk or what to say, because I had no idea what age I ought to act. The gray suit only increased my consternation, as well as adding an additional load to all the burdens that weigh upon me. When I stretched my hand out with the sack in which I had put perfumes and soap and stockings, it seemed to me as if I was giving my daughter Bahija some things I brought back with me from the bakery. Maybe I even intended it that way, because I figured it was inappropriate for a man of seventy to be seen to be in a state, befuddled by young folks. I sat right in the middle of the seat with her, to appear forceful and confident inside the home. She also asked me if I were hungry, so I understood that she was behaving in some way that her age wanted her to behave, and that like me she really didn't know what age she should try to act. When we do not know how we appear to other people who are looking at us, we do not know how to behave. That gray suit added an extra burden for me to contend with. Amid the various comportments that I can recognize as belonging to me, one derived from my tall and lean body from which this suit, rather more sternly, has sprouted.

My brother Hajj Salim didn't get into a flap the way I did,

when he went with his boys to get his second wife from her village. He stayed seated on the low chair at the end of the room while his sons talked to the family. He sat clinched up and hunched over, waiting to get her and get out of there. When they brought them both to his house he wasn't any taller, sitting near to her in one of the cars that suddenly stopped at the *dar* entrance. His patience, uncommunicativeness, and smallness of spirit all served him well, and he didn't let up even climbing up the stairs leading to their house. He seemed short next to her. Moving hastily, his eyes were warily looking about in all directions as if he was on guard against someone lurking nearby, ready to ambush him – and dispossess him of his booty.

I tell my sons I want a domestic servant who will work for me, because no one cooks or washes my clothes. I want a maid, because I myself can't believe how I used to be so fond of marriage. The woman who lived in the house behind my window used to flirt outrageously with me, whenever she saw me looking at her sitting there on her balcony. Her voice would ring out loud and high-pitched, but by the time I was at the point of shouting at her she would change her tone and words, and ask after my health, and about which of my children had come to see me. Sometimes she would mix the joking around with more serious things, so I would understand that someone was watching us or listening to us. I'd move away from the window and hear laughing from two different directions as I closed it. When my son Qassem said he shouldn't introduce people to me I stopped standing at the window. 'A maid,' I told them, 'that's what I need. I'll pay her wages out of the 10,000 pounds that I have. Ugly is all right, but clean.'

The woman kept looking at me while talking to my son's wife, until I jumped up shaking, and shouted in her face. Every time this happened before, she thinks that it is just a matter of a few words before I storm away to my room. But I don't shut up this time. My voice keeps rising and I go on shaking my cane, long after she has fled and gone back inside. Screaming at her, I become unable to stop my memory from dredging up things from the past – and with every new thing I start a fresh torrent of shouting. I can't stop, even as I approach the dark little entryway which partitions off the pantry from the kitchen, or even when I pull up the bed blanket to cover myself.

I expose myself to a rage that my body cannot endure. The thing I cannot shut off after I quiet down is the strong pounding of my blood, crashing from my head to my chest and back again. I don't realize that I made a mistake in taking refuge in my bed until some time after adopting the posture of a sleeping person in it. I become wide awake, to the point that I can see the clear features of men and women nearby, right before my closed eyes. They are clearer and closer than what I'd see with my eyes open with my glasses. Men and women appearing and then fading away; no sooner does one face rise up than it sinks down again. They talk with moving fists and arms as if punishing me for some deed that they all know about. Now that kind of thing comes from excessive wakefulness, and not from falling asleep. I know I made a mistake in going to bed, but I also know that I am going to stay stretched out in it, since I'm there.

The *dar* stays quiet for a couple of hours – an after-effect of my raised voice. That woman keeps her door shut, and my son's wife stays where she is inside the house, no longer visible from the balcony. Even the road that runs parallel to the house from the rear is empty and silent. It occurs to me that I have to get things moving once more, so I go out to the *mastaba* again. Not to sit in my chair, but to move something, anything, in the silent, waiting *dar*.

VI

My son Qassem asked me why I didn't leave the house, since I am able to. He thought I needed to move my feet, to get some exercise, and right away. He turned his body towards the gate and lifted his foot high, as if to dramatize just how easy the first step is. I stayed put, and tilted my head to one side as I looked at him, so that he would realize that his words and movements would never budge me out of the chair. I scratched my neck and then began rubbing my tongue in my mouth, as if I had suddenly discovered some disease in it. He asked me if I was thirsty and brought the *ibreeq* over. I didn't drink anything. I just gazed at the *ibreeq* as it approached me, and then watched it move away again, withdrawn to its original place. I stayed sitting there, bowing my head and grasping the side of the bed with my hand, as if I was experiencing regret for something I had done, but at the same time wanting to blame other people, including my son. But I know it isn't a good idea for me to stay in that position for very long, since his patience might suddenly give way, enabling him to jump up and return to his house. They all force me to keep changing my position in front of them, time and again, so that they don't lose patience, get up, and leave me. I told my son Abu Fayez once that I hadn't slept because of the pain in my chest, and he just barked at me. He said it's because I smoke at this age, and he grabbed my packet of tobacco and hid it from me. I kept silent.

I know it is wrong for me to stay like that for a long time, because he came back and asked again: 'Why don't you go outside?'

'Where?' I ask. He repeats what he has said many times, about how Ali Aqeel's father kept on going out to his terraces and over to his shop, right up to the end of his days. I pointed out to him that Ali Aqeel's father died when he was younger than I am now. He didn't press the point or say that he died when he was 107. All he did was move the tray of food closer to me, in order to get up and go home, after having done his filial duty. I ate straight away, sucking in repeated long breaths of noisy air, as I do when eating.

They see Muhammad Habib in the town square with other men, so they say to me why don't I go visit him in his house? My son Abu Fayez says that the man is prolonging his life by sitting with people. Actually, he sits a little off to the side, outside their circle, and busies himself watching the passers-by while they go on conversing, completely oblivious to his being there. I figured my sons only took notice of him because he stood out, there on his own, and because he appears to be strangely averse to the people sitting there. On those rare and widely-spaced occasions when he would come to my house, I would see that he had nothing to say to me. He would sink into a deep and uninterrupted silence that indicated to me that he had visited quite a few houses before coming to mine. I think he roams around the houses simply to walk, because he never did this before his wife died. He would invite me in as he stood under his archway, and I wondered how he could stand to hold his body so rigidly under those stiff, old-fashioned clothes, which belonged to another era entirely.

On one visit, he calls me in and I keep on walking upon my way, for I feel he is a lazy person and his character has remained unchanged despite all of the years. My son Abu Fayez asks why I don't do what he does – and I'll see in my mind his turban, twisted and pointy in the manner of the old sultans, and his hand, stuck behind the tie of his *sherwaal*. The people of the village would always return from their time in Beirut to find him standing in the same place: under his archway. They greet him with '*Salaam 'alaykom* Abu Habib', and wait for him to return the greeting, which he will do, drawling at length, grandiosely, the way the people of Iraq like to do.

I used to laugh along with everyone else at him, and now my son wants me to be like him. He suggests this because he is not of the same generation. No man appears ridiculous to someone who isn't near him in age. They not only want me to visit him in his house, they want me to spend my time with him doing what he does, as if all that is needed for two men to spend their time together is that they be of the same age.

In those late nights we used to spend in Hajj Ali Farhat's house, we would talk about our boys in Beirut, revealing a secret shared wish that their camaraderie would increase. I would say to my sons when they visited on the *'Id*, 'Let's all go and pay an *'Id* visit to Hajj Ali Farhat and his boys', and I would take the lead as we walked down the street. When we arrived, they would come inside so we looked like a tight-knit family, rather than one that has grown apart as the children became adults, took jobs, and moved away. We would spend just five minutes there and then leave. This family-like comportment we adopted could not endure much longer than that. If it did, maybe we'd have to forgo the happy scene of entering their house together. Just a little bit of time to go in and then come out, that's all. We would regale ourselves until late with recollections of our children who were in Beirut, and nothing would interrupt our talking about them except for Hajj Ali Farhat's getting up to make tea, and my telling Hajja Khadija to wake up. I would say to her: 'come on, get up, Hajja', in order to change the subject, from his endless talk about his bakery in Beirut.

'Did you fall asleep, Hajja?' I'd ask her, and she'd open her eyes suddenly and look towards me, as if trying to question me about something she saw during her nap. I'd kept Hajj Ali Farhat company by talking about the children, I knew he liked nothing more than speaking about them. I'd tell Hajja to wake up, that we must go, although we'd be back the next day. I would walk ahead of her down to the road, telling her to catch up with me, because she takes a long time to gather herself to leave.

I'd always notice what she was doing, and if her hands were empty, I'd leave before her, with Hajj Ali Farhat just starting up on another yarn about his children. He's able to turn any comment said to him into the starting point of a new story.

He wanted me to while away the night hours recollecting the things our sons and their families got up to, just the way my son Abu Fayez wants me to go around with Muhammad Habib, with nothing beyond our ages in common between us. We'd say to him 'Salaam 'alayk, Abu Habib', and he'd let forth his drawn-out and splendid rejoinder. We would all stop walking just long enough to give him our full attention, every ear turned to him.

My son imagines the proximity of our ages alone is enough for us to walk about our town like old buddies. When he suggests this, he is thinking of what childhood peers do when they are grown, and he thinks that we spend our time sitting around doing nothing, just like the grown children do. But when the morning comes upon us we have no idea what we should get up for, so we just sit ourselves down in the same chair we were sitting in yesterday evening. In the morning I simply complete yesterday's vigil, which will only come to an end when the sun warms up around nine o'clock. That's the start of my long day, one in which I do not follow any timings, except having lunch before noon – not so much because I am hungry, but so the day at least has a middle point. The sun gets hot at nine o'clock, as I am sitting and not anticipating anything, so to me it appears to be fixed in place, not moving onwards. Like the gas heater my son Qassem points in my direction and keeps lit in the same place all night. They want Muhammad Habib and me to go out and play. We can roam the streets and alleys of the town together, and both stop at various points on the way to double-check something which we think at first glance to be something else. We will both be bewildered by it, Muhammad Habib and I, and each one of us will have an opinion, and we make bets as we get closer, only to find that it is some third thing we didn't consider as a possibility. We will play in the town so that we can eat lunch at lunch time, and not before that. They yell out to their children from the floor above me, and the *dar* soon becomes void of them. I complained to Qassem that the children shout and yell all day. But I stay seated there with them, nothing separating us apart from the edge of the *mastaba* – four steps above the courtyard of the *dar*. Just the kids and I down here; their parents upstairs hear only our faint voices.

There are lots of people in the *dar*, even children I don't know, it's like they spontaneously sprung to life out of the collection of people that never stops flowing from the top floor. I see a boy who has an air about him that is completely different from any of our expressions, and gesture to him to come closer. He turns his back and waits a short while before being swept away from me by a game the other children draw him into. The children of the woman who lives in the top story of Hajj Salim's house maintain their wariness towards me; if my glance falls on one of them he will stop his playing and take a step or two away from the bunch, just in case. I can see his mother's hatred for me in his darkening gaunt face; he doesn't shift his eyes from me until he has stared at great length at my face. Qassem tells me that I am always sitting on my *mastaba* right in front of them, as if he wants me to hide myself away in the dark sunless space between the pantry and the storage attic. I tell him I am not talking about his children, but about other people's children, among whom there are some I don't know.

There are lots of people in the *dar*, and I don't scare any of them except for the children of the woman on the top floor of my brother Hajj Salim's house. But I don't even raise my voice at them until the evening, by which time my cool has run out and I can't stand seeing them any longer. Then they'll stop playing for a moment, until one of our children throws a ball to another standing in front of him. My son Abu Fayez wants me to go out and about and doesn't realize that I spent an entire year retreating back to the house from the town square that lies behind the driveway. I had begun putting that quizzical smile on my face that absorbs the talk of the folks who sit in the square, and I shift my eyes around following the talk as it moves between them. I act like I only sit with them to watch and listen, so they will forget that I am there.

Muhammad Habib is content with that, but me, no. I started bringing my chair over with me, I'd sit apart at the beginning of the driveway entrance, yet still looking out onto the square and the shop. Under my daughter's house, to my right at the very end of the driveway, lies the big gateway of our *dar*. The more time I spent out there, the more I found myself moving my chair closer to my house, until after a year had gone by I no longer moved it at all from its place on the *mastaba*. My son Abu Fayez still wants me to go to Muhammad Habib's house and sit talking with him under the archway of his house, where we used to laugh at him in his neat outfit, so carefully wrapped all around him.

Muhammad Habib and I used to sit under the arch of his

entranceway. We spent time together in order to set morning apart from noontime. We'd split up at lunch to eat at our own homes. I didn't stop going out to my lands because of fatigue, but rather because they kept telling me it wasn't fitting for me to work at my age. I was over eighty then, although both my legs were still strong. I killed the tortoise that had scared my son's son in the terraces. I pounded it with a stone until its back was pulverized and the blood appeared, deep red, as if it had a tender soul under its corrugated skin. I passed the age of eighty, but I could still lift stones so high that my shirt nearly split at the armpit. They said it wasn't right for me to work, and that the small amount of yield I got in return wasn't worth the effort of going to the fields. I knew that they didn't tell me this to take a burden off my shoulders, but to get me off the land and leave it to them. How quickly they take hold of any place I stop going to; they all know their inheritance – who gets what – so nobody cares if I give something to someone else. They forced me out of the piece of land that I was keeping for myself, and I didn't ask them what I should do with the power that was still in my body, or how I was meant to keep myself in the house. Abu Fayez stood with them, apparently the leader, so that I would understand that they had decided on this matter all together before coming to me. They always came together when they wanted something. It wasn't very long after I left the Beirut bakery that this became the norm. My last day in the bakery, after I'd signed it over to them, they just stood there at my hands, submissively and obediently, waiting for me to gather my few things from the countertop. I was no less vigorous than them when I left the bakery, but I didn't yet realize that the person who we obey is the one standing at his counter. Back in the town I ask how the bakery is doing, and they relate small pieces of news, say something about a distant relative who dropped in to visit, or about the owners of nearby shops – as if what is happening with its customers or who is coming to its till is of no concern to me. They'll tell me news of visitors and neighbors, and I will content myself with what they tell me, just the way Hajja Khadija used to satisfy herself when I replied to her with words that let her know that the matter was not her business. The Beirut bakery gives the 'last say' in the family to whoever runs it, and I didn't realize this until I had removed my things from it and left for the village. Their expressions changed, and they began to knit their brows in front of me.

They wouldn't try to clear their faces of the exhaustion they intentionally adopted, knowing that weary features distinguish those who give orders from those who carry them out. I said to one of them, 'Why are you so overburdened and worried like this?' His look of weariness and apprehension only intensified. Soon this was the only look I saw when meeting up with them, so much so that on each occasion it seemed that they were training for manliness in front of me. We exchanged roles and demeanors after my exit from the Beirut bakery. They began to look like they were thinking of matters in which we shared no mutual concern. Their faces looked distant and foreign, and seemed to draw them back to the business in Beirut.

I know they put on these looks of tiredness when they

come to me, in order to consolidate their ownership and not have it divested from them. After I gave them the bakery I went over to it a number of times. I would begin my visit by inspecting its stocks and the bread, as if to remind them that they were managing work that belongs to me. I strolled around the premises, poked my nose into every corner, and picked up scraps of bread and paper to throw away in the big trash barrel under the stairs up to its storage attic. I'd cast my eyes over the oven and tap the tiles with the baker's peel. I wouldn't remind them they were managing a business that belonged to me in order not to diminish their authority in front of the bakery workers. I'd stand behind the till and take the money from customers like I'd done for years. I'd ask one of my boys what the price on the *ka'ak* was that day and he'd quickly step in front of me, pushing me away, taking over the transaction.

They play games with me as well. They try to make me understand that many things have changed since I left. Customers I've never seen before come in, and the boys have quick conversations with them, leaving me wondering how I should behave. I count the change in my head at times and remember how my brother Hajj Salim was so slow-moving with his customers. When I came down to Beirut on another occasion, I know, before even stepping over the threshold of the bakery, that I need to sit down on the chair that's in the corner and not leave it – not only because of what happened on my previous visit, but because I infer that I am a low-status visitor, due to my ill-fitting clothes. In Beirut I get confused, as if I hadn't lived there and had never established bakeries there. The suit that I wear on my body seems to have become heavy, and full of the smells of the home town. I see that the first thing I need to do is to compose myself and bring my body and clothes into sync. I sit in silence in the chair in the corner and content myself – there inside the bakery where the workers are – with simply looking on. I sit waiting for one of them to end his workday and give me a ride to his house. In the last hours of these waiting periods I sometimes went out onto the street to wait near the car, in the hope that this might hurry up the departure, and accepting the fact that I have nothing left of my bakery in my hands beyond the 500 pounds they give me monthly as spending money.

Then, they would take me to their house where they go to sleep a few minutes after arriving. In the house that I left to my daughter, they'll leave me with her alone and go off to take care of their business. She'll be in the kitchen so I will call her and wait a while until she comes. I'll ask her to flip the channels on the radio, which exasperates her and makes her shake it with both hands as if she wanted to shake something out of it. Whenever her husband returned from his work he'd make me feel like I was sitting in his chair, and not in my own home. They take over the place just as soon as I move out of it. They left me nothing in Beirut beyond touring around their houses, shifting from one to the other just to sit with their women and children. I go down some stairs and climb up others, and can never tell if they are more pleased with my leaving their houses or setting foot in them. My son would climb the stairs behind me, and at the top I'll see his wife standing at the door with her children, waiting.

It is a reception that doesn't last very long, and time starts to drag the minute I choose a place to settle down.

I gather my things around me in the bed or on the couch and yell at them, while they are busy with their work. Time moves slowly from the instant I sit down, and I begin right away to think of moving to another house. I had nothing left in Beirut but to roam the streets setting their houses apart from each other, and climb the stairs leading up to them. Sayyid Mahdi told me once that anyone who bequeaths his wealth to his children while yet alive won't be able to stand sitting around with them any more. I didn't pay him any heed; I kept giving my possessions to them, each and every time just to revive a little of the old intimacy, if only for a week or two.

I'd walk in their midst and take them all around my plots of land, spread about the limits of town. I'd draw them the boundaries that set my property off from others and I'd be very deliberate about pointing out the lines and walking along them, as if to prolong the time that they were silent in my presence.

Although I didn't heed his advice on this matter, I'd often ask Sayyid Mahdi questions like 'How did your father spend his last days?' 'Alone and bored', he would answer. When asked a year before his own death why he too was 'alone and bored', he said that everyone he ever knew had died. That day I realized that religiously-inclined men become companions and friends of people like us and don't sit at home waiting for someone to come along to ask after them. I asked him, 'Why didn't you get to know other people after they died?' At the time I was still in possession of my property and had my sons around. And that's when he said: 'Don't give them an inheritance.' I thought it was because he was afraid of their repudiating me; he always generalized about folks rather than taking the trouble to notice the differences that existed between them. He talked about them as a block, when he was preaching in those sermons he gave in the Husseiniyah, and he saw them as really living one and the same life, and dying one and the same death.

When my boys evicted me from the last piece of land I had left, the one I was holding for myself, they said it was because they didn't feel it was right for me to work at my age. My eldest son's voice, scolding and determined, made me feel that I had been caught sneaking out onto the land secretly. All the boys stood there together, it was the same united stand they took the day they found out about my going to Marwaniyah to visit that woman. And it was the same tone that Abu Fayez used to tell me that I had to stop being afraid of dying. My son screwed up his face in the fullest frown he could muster, and borrowed an accent from someone I didn't know to diminish anything I might say or any familiar look I might send his way. The exact same tone and posture, as if all of my mistakes – the only thing I am capable of – are equivalent in their offensiveness. Or as if I had done some hugely reprehensible, unmentionable deed that they castigate me for whenever they get the chance. I'm at a loss and don't know what to do with my time, knowing that I will really and truly get sick if I treat myself the way a sick person is treated. I eat just very light food, distributing the meals over a long lifetime. Setting down the plate of *labneh* that I have prepared for my dinner I imagine that I am holding off things that were going to happen to me. But what do I do after a *labneh* dinner? And what do I do the day after? Two weeks later I'll emerge after completely forgetting my body and diet. I'll light up a cigarette with my trembling fingers, and the smoke flows out like it would from an old rotting and perforated smokestack. I'll go back to it after a few weeks or a month of quitting. I used to toss the pack away unfinished, and say to it 'Go away for two months', or 'Go away for six months'. They say that's harder than just quitting cold turkey.

I was known, after all, for my willpower. That helped me pass the time lightly. It is easy for me to take control of my smoking; how quickly a man adopts qualities that are attributed to him. As I've said, that's how I was able to continue going down into the well into my seventies, not only out of my strength, but also out of fear of its darkness and depth. When I dove down under the water, I knew it was the same water I drink. The terror of the darkness I could manage by fixing my heart firmly in place. I had learned the Prophet's saying from Sayyid Mahdi's sermons: 'If you are afraid of something, jump into it.' So I asked him when he came down off the *minbar* of the Husseiniyah: 'What about dying, should we jump into it, Sayyid Mahdi?'

I asked him because I really wasn't afraid of anything apart from it. Death itself doesn't frighten me, since it can come to us when we stretch out on our beds. Real and true death, the kind our parents died, is not the same as the one we know that brings on wailing and bloody tears, or comes upon us like a stab in the waist, as we are standing. I don't feel frightened of that, since it can take place with the light of day still strong around us, and will be over as soon as our bodies gurgle and collapse to the ground. What I mean is the fear of what dead folks live with in their graves, of the djinns and the angels that are hovering over them. I throw them down into the pit of the well with the light I have in my hand, and they scatter and disappear. The water regains its human character when its darkness is cast away. I swim in it without being afraid of the stagnant sounds that rise from my body's splashing against it, while they are all up there, all worked-up and scared.

I am afraid of the death that my son Abu Fayez tells me to stop being afraid of, because someone like me in their ninety-forth year is no longer going to die with raging and bleeding. There are no looming dangers, and there are no enemies about to ambush me in the narrow spaces between the kitchen and the bed and the *mastaba*. They evicted me from my house and I never asked them what I am supposed to do with my fear – these are the kinds of things that are not said. And if I did say them, they wouldn't get anything out of Abu Fayez beyond a scornful echo of the words which he would mix into the scowl that he concentrates between his lips and teeth. He'll let me understand that now he can see that my fear of death has been confirmed. He told me that we are all going to die, and that he himself was going to die. I just stayed there silently stretched out on my bed. He wants me to surrender to my death and to accept it, simply because it is inevitable, and it is going to happen.

He always picks a time when I am unwell to explain to me just how easy a thing death is. He takes me by the hand and pulls my sick body along to meet it. He believes he is helping me, since he thinks that the only thing standing between me and my dying is my fear and my cussedness. I tell him to go to Nabatiyah and get me the doctor; he says the doctors have work on others besides me to attend to. I ask myself if he really does not fear death, I mean his death and not the death he is talking about, about which he knows nothing – except that the souls rise up from the bodies.

He raises his hand, fingers held closely together, from the middle of his chest to the top of his head, thinking that this explains how easily and lightly – just so – they rise up. As if I am not his father.

When my illness overwhelms me he stands among my visitors and relates to them what happened last night, without checking to see if I might have passed out or if I am hearing what he is saying. He tells them what I did, and where I felt the pain, without even trying to keep his voice down. I hear it well. Sometimes I will let out a groan or open my eyes and pick him out from among the bunch. He'll tell them I opened my eyes and he takes a step towards me. He pulls the blanket up to my chin and waits over me for a long time, then goes back to talking with them. He figures my sickness has taken complete hold of me, that my soul has become faint and slight as a result, and that I am no longer able to perceive what comes to my ears. As if I am not his father. He talks of my actions and my pains as if I was a broken-down machine, and he nods his head towards me when the discussion pushes him to point me out. His nodding gesture moves swiftly upwards, meaning I am over there sleeping. Perhaps he is pushing me and my bed a bit further to the rear, and increasing his renouncement of me and his distance. I move my tongue in my mouth, and the parched sound of my throat reaches their ears. I know that they all have directed their eyes towards me, because in that instant the talk between them ceases. They are all standing, and that means that they see that my condition has taken a turn for the worse and that my death is imminent. They are all watching at every moment, so that they can distinguish its arrival clearly.

It was an illness, not the throes of death.

I get up from it, feeble and spent, colorless. I move dizzily to my chair on the *mastaba*, my eyes looking right and left. But I get there. My son's wife will sleep an extra two hours when she realizes that I have recovered this time as well. She'll say to her children in an exasperated tone that she will end up dying before me, and that Azraa'eel has no power over me. The dizziness in my head clears away a few minutes after sitting down. I lift my hand up to the hair of my beard – it has grown long during my illness – and remember the road to the barbershop in Nabatiyah. I raise the other hand and place it on the edge of the *mastaba*. I stretch it forward so that they see it, and will send my son to make tea for me.

VII

Qassem says that I wake them by playing the Qur'anic recitation too loud, which I do from daybreak. They grumble in their households, and apparently can't deafen their ears to the sound coming up from below, though they have no problem doing this when their children yell and scream in the *dar*. They ṣaid it did no good for them to bury their heads under their pillows, and no amount of insisting could get sleep to stay in their bodies. But this is all I have left, in terms of remembering God, since I broke off praying two or three years ago. As for fasting in Ramadan, I have never been able to make it through the entire month. Because of boredom, not hunger. I could never stand to just sit around waiting for something or someone. I'd say: 'Get up and give me the food, Hajja.' She'd stand for a while in hesitation, before turning to head back to the kitchen.

I'd turn the radio up all the way, and bring it out with me from the room, setting it down on the edge of the *mastaba*. That's what I'd do in offering my prayers, in the middle of the room, beginning them with a loud voice with which I would forget Hajja Khadija praying in her room. She would always prolong the phase, sitting on her prayer rug, and I figured that was due to her slowness in reciting the verses. She was slow in her praying the same way she was slow in her work. I would finish putting on all of my clothes, and she would still be sitting in prayer.

I would sometimes step in front of her and wave, whereupon she adopted a demeanor of piety and contemplation, as if she was enjoying the meanings of the words in the verses that I knew she didn't understand. She read the Qur'an but didn't understand the meaning. When I bought the *aya kabeera* for her, I said, 'Read it, Hajja'. I stared at her for a while the way schoolboys do.

'Verily we have ... *fatahna laka fathan mubeenan*,' she read out loud. I asked her what '*fatahna laka fathan mubeenan*' means, and she answered that Allah opened a clear door for the Prophet. 'So why is it a verse?' I asked.

She'd be on her prayer rug reciting the words of the *ayat* at her leisurely pace, even stopping between one word and the next. She believed this is a sign of extreme devotion. When I'd see her really going overboard I'd interrupt and ask, 'Where did you put my socks? What have you done with them?' She'd turn her head from right to left before getting up slowly and grumbling as she walked to the closet.

She also told me I put the radio on too loud, and she drew courage from the children when they visited on summer holiday. She'd climb the stairs to them whenever she felt they were awake, and she'd stay the whole morning up there. I'd call her from below two or three times until she heard me. When she appeared, coming down the stairs, I'd raise my voice, so they'd hear me upstairs, and stick their heads out from the balcony to see what I might do. I'd only yell at her but not do anything else. Not for fear of them, but afraid of her silence which weighed down on me every time I had the urge to raise a fist to her. It is as if she protected herself with the piety of her father, who spent such a long time dying. She'd appear as if she was forced to reside in my house, and would always make me think that she silently compared her life with me to that in her father's house.

To be honest, I do turn the radio on high to wake them up. I want them to fidget in their beds, where they are trying not to raise their voices and keep their grumbling from my ears. This is all that is left of my influence on the household. I turn up the radio full blast to test my authority; every time I turn it up I wait for someone to yell at me. My son waited for me to finish eating to spring it on me. I answered it was the Qur'anic recitation, that it was God speaking and they needed to listen to *Him*. Qassem gave me a look as if to say, 'Come on, we all know you are no pious hermit'. Neither of us is very religious, for that matter. He is almost sixty and his praying is still haphazard. Faith comes to him in strong gusts and then fades away, just the same way as with my giving up smoking. He projects his voice loud and strong on the prayer rug, as if he is making up for past periods when he was preoccupied and neglecting his faith. No, I am not pious and neither are any of my children. I certainly can't imagine my eldest son standing humbly at the disposal of his Lord, and neither can anyone else. His tone of voice and the scowl on his lips and teeth seem to have prepared him for something different. I used to take them to the bakeries when they were still small, so it was not easy for them to learn anything from the stories of the religious sheikhs. I told myself that they had to get used to working or they would idle away their lives as charlatans. In the house I took up in Nabatiyah I would say to my wife: 'Read the Qur'an to them', but she wouldn't do it. She seemed to have learned it only to be able to say she had, if asked.

She'd open it up and read an *ayah* or two before seeing who was around her, gazing at each one in turn as if waiting for somebody to ask her to read another page. Her voice came out strangely, as if she was mimicking people from another village. I'd go along with them and quiz her as well: 'Read to them', I'd tell her, in order to see if she looked as strange as she sounded. Through sheer piety her father could will his own soul to take leave of his body. He just put his hand on his stomach and said to it: 'You're here,' and then moved his hand upwards, bringing it to his chest, adding 'Well done, well done'. He'd sit on his bed, supporting his back against the wall. I'd ask him, 'What is your will and testament, uncle?' He asked me to take care of the two girls, because 'a boy knows how to take care of himself'. Then he started to repeat, 'Come on out, bless you, come out', to coax his soul out of his chest, where, recalcitrant, it had settled.

'And the house?' I asked, but he didn't answer. 'Ok then, the land, who gets the land?' He wasn't looking at me or anyone sitting around him. His face grew rosier, as if to beautify the last image there would be of his face before he died. He didn't dally much with his property in his life, either, and would sell bits of it off as if he would not be losing anything and would never miss it. 'What do we do with the house in Kawthariyah?' I asked him. He appeared delighted with the control he had exerted upon his life. He said, 'Go on, blessed one', pronouncing the utterance from the front of his mouth as if it were a tiny spit of air. I went out to where Hajja Khadija waited with the women. She sat right in the middle of them, inclining her head to one side with her eyes closed, as if inventorying the memories appearing in her mind's eye.

I turn the radio up as far as it can go to get them up and out of their beds and pillows, because their voices kept coming down to me until midnight. That's the other reason I do it. I leave the light on because I know that I will never fall asleep as long as I am hearing their voices rising sharp and loud like that, as they go about cursing someone whose name came up during the evening. I get up from my bed to answer needs that, through their unrelenting insistence, exhaust me. Their voices subside for a while and then start rising once again. I think that she must have brought them coffee for the fourth time. She comes out of the kitchen with it and hastens to the balcony to prolong their evening an additional hour. I didn't say to my son, when he came to me about my radio, 'So let them lower their voices in the night time' because he will never believe that they wear me out. He thinks my hearing is weak, like my sight. He also thinks that they both get weaker with each passing day. I see him peering at me upon his return from work, looking like he is trying to determine just how much more I have lost. They add years to my age with every passing month and they treat me according to the old age they have prematurely accorded to me. Not one of them believes that I can remain in the same condition over two consecutive visits. They think they are winning this game, wearing me down, and this attitude doesn't dissipate after I recover from my illnesses. They are impatient. The illness breeds no new sympathy or compassion.

The tone of Abu Fayez's voice when I moaned in my bed is not altered in any way by my sitting on the *mastaba* after my recovery. He acts like it was a round in a competition he's won against me. He's waiting to put on his frowning face when I ask for something, or complain. My son Qassem brings me sick people's food intended to restore one to health but that no one can stand to eat. I say to him, 'I'm fine now, I've recovered', and he gets confused, unsure of what to do with the little plate in his hands.

To them, there is no recovery from an illness; it is an escape from the jaws of death. From the minute I resume getting out of bed and going outside, the men stop coming around to my house. They need a more powerful occasion than a passing illness to gather together around one of my sons and adopt their silent comportment of grief. They didn't come to the clinic where I stayed many days during my illness, but they are ready to come to the room to keep my sons from being alone there with death.

They get the better of me in this round of sickness. They think me no longer worthy of the compassion heaped on the dying. If I had died the compassion would have been ladled out in soothing heaps. By recovering, I snuck up on them like an adversary from behind. They figure that I escaped death through some kind of unseemly cunning, a trickery that was inappropriate for someone my age. They wanted me to arrive at death through my illness, so as not to undermine the feelings of compassion they lavished upon me while I was stretched out on the bed. I had led them into an ambush, and succeeded in getting them to fall into it. I know I am supposed to come across as a victim, both of my illness and my recovery from it. Qassem asked if anything was still giving me pain, so I know they expect me to make noises to signal that I am hurting. But it is a dull, tolerable pain. I gesture to the sofa and then to Abu Fayez as if to apologize for his being so busy with me. I say to Qassem, 'Have a seat', and mimic their tired faces.

Not only do I not turn down the radio, I conceal it. It's the only form of remembrance of Allah left for me to depend upon for my repentance. I used to say to Hajja Khadija: 'What should I seek repentance for, when I haven't killed anyone?' She would keep silent, not finding anything to say in one quick sentence. She would've thought of her sister Fatima who could never forgive me, of my hatred for my brother Hajj Salim, and of the paucity of my connection to religion. And she would think of other things such as the destruction I wrought on the entrails of cats or my hanging a verse from the Qur'an on the wall of the old room to cover up the gap where weapons were stashed.

She even thought I should atone for my loud voice, for forcing my body to stay strong and vigorous, and for going down into the well at the age of seventy. She couldn't find one single thing to say because as she saw it there was unbelief and profanity in everything that does not amount to spending one's life waiting for death, or adhering to the strict implementation of religious duties for fear of what the afterlife might bring. I would turn the radio up all the way and keep myself alert to who is in the house around me. I'd hear whoever it may be and never bow my head or my back, and look like I am about to submit my body to the angels. That's the way Fatima looked when she did her ablutions for the dawn prayer. Hajja Khadija said that I wash my hands and arms during my prayer ablutions as if I am rolling up my sleeves to fight with someone. All of this required repentance in her eyes, even more than my actual deeds – she really didn't know how to determine which of those was the most offensive and therefore needed the quickest atonement. I'd stand erect on my prayer rug.

The booming sound of my prayers would frighten her, as if my only purpose in reciting a prayer or a verse was to transmit panic and alarm into her heart. That's the way my body and my voice are, and that's also the way my heart is. I turn up the sound of the Qur'an being recited every day, as if expecting forgiveness to arrive from the sheer length of time spent listening to it. I turn it as far up as it can go so that they can hear it loud and clear way up there on the top floor. I distribute passages of the Qur'an among them all, the same way a wealthy person might pass bread around to the needy. I tell myself this is the speech of God Himself, so let them listen to it. I go on turning the radio until it finds the orientation at which it works its loudest. I don't do anything to repent since that takes more time than I have left. 'That alone deserves repentance', Hajja Khadija would've said if she'd heard what I was saying.

Most put their bodies on a path in order to submit to a higher power that might take pity upon them and be compassionate. As for me, well God left me to take care of matters myself. I walk alone along the long *mastaba* as if I am trying to shove people away with my feet. They scatter like birds from my approaching footsteps. The woman closes her door and windows to put more distance between herself, her children, and me. And that other woman, the one my brother Hajj Salim let rent the separate room: I never saw her laugh a single time. I drive them off, back to their houses so that I can extend my authority over the entire *dar*. I only let them have a space they can close a door upon. Their footsteps traverse the distance to their space from the big entryway, and they keep their heads down as if their glances might bring peril upon them.

I shut off the sound of the radio and wait for the break of the dawn light, moving back and forth from the bed to the *mastaba* and the wash basin that is there at the end. A hot breath of wind flies up around me and I wonder where such heat could come from so early in the morning. I rise, and go to the bed, lie down, and cover myself with the blanket. I turn off the radio and wait for the break of dawn. I immediately take up the posture of someone who is asleep, and start to deaden my excessive wakefulness by thinking of the bodies that come to my mind as floating lightly, and by thinking of the faces one by one, and talking without cessation. I fall into sleep as if I had cast myself off from a high place. The faces draw me further downwards, incrementally over slight distances, until I come to a stop suddenly, when, all in one instant, the features and expressions become frightening. They take on increasingly bizarre shapes as I come nearer to what – in my hallucination – must be the bottom of the pit. I open my eyes to cast away the bits of the bodies that have stuck to me, and discover that I am wide awake. These imaginings wore me out completely, but without placing me on the road to sleep. I throw the blanket off and lift my head and back off the bed, as if I were responding to a sudden surprise that didn't frighten me. I return to where I was before on the *mastaba*. I sit on my chair, and then a thick cloud of hot air passes over me, warming me. The light is starting to come up, faintly, but just enough to reassure me that the heat is from a distant burning fire, rather than out of nowhere like a fever from a diseased body.

VIII

He said to me, after running down the stairs, that I'd lived out my own lifetime and that of others as well, and that I had to die. His voice was louder and stronger than mine, as I had worn mine out yelling at the kids all afternoon. He began pumping his hand up and down, still shouting at me, as if he wanted to pound me with his fist. Then he said I have to give people a break. The stairway, over which he towered, was all that kept us apart. On their balcony his mother stood silently, observant, with a demeanor that seemed to encourage him to ramp up his anger in his bellowing voice. That woman living on the top floor of my brother Hajj Salim's house also came out. The kids in the *dar* scurried towards the water basins to get a better view, and also to allow an easy escape, if things went too far.

He shut me up. I felt confused, exposed, and at a loss there in the open, empty courtyard, their balconies towering above me. Perhaps I was waiting for him to finish his ranting so I could return to my room. He kept pumping his hand up and down, but did not come any closer to me. I no longer comprehended anything he said apart from the stream of expletives gushing out between his lecturing. He spat them out passionately, repeating those he was particularly pleased with a few times more.

This was the grandson to whom I gave 100 pounds so he'd agree to get a haircut. I used to cook for him, the type of meals Hajja Khadija would've spent two days preparing. I'd step over the bedding I laid out for him near my bed, and he'd wake up. I'd ask him, 'What will you eat today?', and he'd rattle off names of complicated dishes, while stretching in his bed and laughing to suggest that it was silly to think that we could make anything edible. He'd say to me, 'Come down, grandpa, it's my turn', and I would climb off the donkey so he could get on top. He'd give up asking me if Kawthariyah was far away when he rode up there. I walked behind him pulling the cow along with my hand. 'Ride on top of it, grandpa, climb on the cow', he'd say and laugh happily whenever I was playful. The words came lightly out of his mouth, without leaving any trace behind in his heart. I even let him watch the bull mount our cow, thinking that his laughter would wash away the squalidness and shame of the scene.

At the steps, I continued to stand there, glaring at him, causing him to yell louder and louder. Soon, I know, they'll take him off to class amid an uproar, a part of the plot they're hatching over their numerous pots of coffee. When I finally try to respond to his yelling, nothing works until I use my loudest voice, which I deliberately raise to match his decibel level. I fire the words from my mouth like cannonballs, though my heart is neutral, like someone who's stumbled into a brawl with a person he does not despise. He continued and

I finally shut up again, though I continued to stand there, and continued to glare, not knowing what else to say. They all stood there on their long balcony, neither trying to get him to quiet down nor sending anyone to lead me away. They seemed safe in the knowledge that he would not go beyond this degree of confrontation, a degree they probably had agreed upon over their cups of coffee. He whirled around and climbed up to the house, silently, taking his time, so that they could congratulate him at the top of the stairs.

There were a lot of them up there, including guests from Beirut. There were so many of them that their cars didn't leave any space for anyone coming along to squeeze by to the large doorway. I told the littlest one of them, Ahmad, to go and play cards with his friends away from my window, and he just hunkered down to stay in his place. When they win a round with me they never revert to the manner they maintained previously. It is a battle and they hold onto conquered territory. I let out just one shout at Ahmad and then went to my bed. Their voices reached me from places within the house where they never had before. This multitude of guests filled every crevice. They spilled into the filthy cow shed, and put chairs on the landings of the narrow winding staircase. I am on tenterhooks when there are large numbers of them like this, and probably seem like a child misbehaving in front of unexpected guests. I spend a long and exhausting day monitoring their jabbering. Ahmad slapped the table with the whole of his hand as he dealt out the cards, wanting me to hear the sound of his impetuousness. Whenever they called to one another from the balcony their voices rang out loudly.

The house frothed over with so many of them. Every once in a while one of them cast a challenging glance down at the furthest reach of my *mastaba* and stairway.

My family is always ready to put on the raucous and boisterous welcome they believe is the due of all guests. The entire village is, for that matter. Folks may even fight just to please the guests, and light off firecrackers on the road to the mosque behind their houses. Their loud screeching voices ring out as if engaged in combat. They seemed about to jump down barefoot from the high wall of their house to greet their guests. They're indistinguishable, one from the other, when they are together. The one who'd insulted me ran quickly past my window so I wouldn't see him. If I call out to him while he is still at the bottom of the stairs he'll come back with his head lowered and say that he thought I was asleep. Two minutes, and he's off again. But he will have spent them making polite small talk and asking about my health. I laugh and try to bring him closer and have him linger longer, and say: 'Come and sit on the bed near me'. When he gets up to go he promises me he'll come back. Just two minutes, but in those two minutes I will have singled him out and cut him down to his former size once again. When one of them is with me all alone, he changes his manner, so as to suggest that if afterwards he shrinks away from me or raises his voice against me, it would only be to fit in with the others.

He told me, standing there on the stairs, that I bothered all of them because I couldn't seem to leave anyone alone. It was as if they had elected him their representative. They keep mounting these confrontations, rushing to prepare the next one like they are pressing towards a finish line.

I resigned myself to this when the eldest son also screamed at me. I put my hand on my heart and gasped in pain, making suffocating sounds, swaying on the verge of collapse. That wasn't entirely concocted, since groaning and swaying come easy to me, and my voice and body are right in step with whatever I do. My hand lifted towards my chest as if warding off some real agony, and out comes the gasping, of its own accord. I sometimes don't know if I can bring to a halt what I've started, and fear I might actually collapse. Perhaps that is the true cause of fatal strokes: suggestion. I started calling out for my father in my calculated agonizing. I say: 'Oh daddy', and squeeze my eyes shut tight. I heard little Ahmad tell them I was doing this to frighten them. His older brother stopped shouting and began to look at me closely to see if a stroke had really come upon me. He lifted his face close to mine, pale, hesitant, and bewildered, torn between believing and disbelieving my ordeal. When I let out a huge moan he ran towards me, stretching his hands out to catch me. His brothers ran down the stairs, followed by others, not to help, but to get a better view of the action. One of them finally did take me from his brother and began to massage my hands and my heart with such force that I bounced right up onto my feet, lifting my head up and looking around at the people, as if I'd awoken from a 100-year nap.

There were a lot of them upstairs. They made way on either side of the balcony so that they could bring me up there for examination, to see if I had really had a stroke.

They peered at me with curious, skeptical eyes. They brought me hastily to the far end of the balcony and left me standing there, propping myself up with my cane, making eye contact with no one, while debating amongst themselves which chair would be best. Finally, the eldest, the one who had shouted at me, brought the large chair and asked me to wait as he unbuttoned my shirt, then re-buttoned it in the correct order. I am not sure if I'd buttoned it wrong that morning or if this happened while they were squeezing my chest in the courtyard. He refastened it slowly, deliberately, with two carefully positioned synchronized hands.

Ahmad, sure that I was not suffering from anything at all, looked about smiling; doing whatever was asked of him with playfully exaggerated hesitation. They sat around me and stretched their necks to get a closer look. I kept quiet among them, thinking that anything I might say would give me away and cause them to scatter. I let out long raspy breaths that sped up whenever the crowd grew quiet, like a wave of little strokes that washed over me, then receded, as my breathing settled from its pentacle of crisis to its normal pace. I moved my tongue around in my mouth to make a sound of parched dryness. They brought me a glass of water, thinking that I wouldn't be strong enough to hold the *ibreeq* in my two trembling hands. The one who'd shouted at me brought the glass to my mouth, holding it by his fingertips, conveying the smallness of the glass and the purity of its water. He made his hands delicate and attentive, as if hoping that they would do no harm to me in my weakened and fragile condition. He even peeled a pear for me and divided it into little pieces which he put on a plate in front of me. The pieces slid between his fingers as he gave them all his attention, using the task as an excuse for not talking to me. Their mother did not emerge from the kitchen. I figured that she was telling all the women that I had tricked them and they were dumb enough to fall for it. The eldest said, 'Eat this, granddad, eat', and pushed the plate of pear slices towards me. I showed him my two trembling hands. He had divided the pear into little pieces, perhaps so they would leave their mark on my heart before getting to my stomach. He brought his fingers close to my mouth and popped in the first little morsel of pear. I started looking pained as I gulped it down, although I accepted the second morsel too. I even stretched my head forward and opened my mouth ahead of the next slice, to let him know that the pear was providing me with some benefit.

I start shifting about to get up and they sit me back down. I sat up again after finishing the pear. They had become distracted, talking to their guests, so I told them that I had to go back down to my house. The older one told me to sit back down and then returned to his conversation, when I did. I turned to him and asked, 'Where are these guests from?' He said they were his brother's neighbors. Two women stood with their backs stuck against the wall, and they never looked at me again once they confirmed I could eat. The two of them would pick up things and turn them about in their hands, and bring them close to their faces, as if they were clothes that they were darning. The one on my side talked whenever someone spoke to her and laughed afterwards, as if she just answered a riddle or succeeded in solving a simple puzzle.

And they all laughed with her. They love the country towns and visit them from Beirut as often as possible. They say it's because of the clean air. 'It's as good as fresh farm eggs', they say. They take in long, deep breaths as they climb out of their cars. Anyone with them would imagine that they can really smell and taste the air, and that they can distinguish its various types. The older grandson sitting next to me prompts the woman so that the others keep laughing at her talk. She plays along with him in that respect, for she will go quiet all of a sudden and start staring at her hands, in preparation for a new question. I asked Ahmad if they were Muslim, but he didn't answer. He was convinced that I was just fine and that there was nothing bothering me, and that I had faked the stroke. I knew I would not risk giving myself away to him. His eyes flashed with alarm that I was inviting him to be an accomplice. I told him, 'It's better for me to get up, grandson', and I made two attempts to move out of my chair, but without success. The eldest said, 'Sit down, grandpa', and stood up to grab my hand. I stood for a while, allowing the dizziness in my head to subside. I pounded my cane hard on the floor just one time, and started walking, with Ahmad escorting me one step behind.

They don't accept that I won this round. I was still feeling for the last step when Ahmad's laugh rang out. He peered at them from the edge of the balcony. It occurred to me that I ought to yell at him from where I was, right underneath him, but I continued my way, realizing it would be better just to leave things as they were. I then knew they hadn't believed that I was having a stroke to the extent that I thought they had, and I knew that they would wait a while before they would see his laugh as the occasion for embarrassment. I kept on my way to my bed, squinting and clinching my jaws shut, as if to crush this incident that was planted in my head like a bitter, poisonous seed. I knew, as I stretched out on the bed, that they would take turns mimicking my stroke and my recovery on the balcony. Ahmad will sit on the chair that I was sitting in and stretch his fist forward, like he's holding my cane. He will pull his head backwards and stare at each of them; then he'll stretch it forward and pucker his lips to mock my eating of the pear slices. His mother will come out of the kitchen to laugh with him, and they will all be ready to turn away from the woman who had been entertaining them and keeping them laughing, except that she herself will get up, in the throes of their hilarity and uproar, to imitate my stroke and start swaying and shaking her head in all directions, as if she is hurrying to bring to an end a fast dance. They laugh for her too, and no one will get up to stop them and tell them that I am their grandfather, since they will stop at nothing when they have a chance for a few good laughs.

I won't say anything about this to their father when he arrives. He won't do anything for me. When their eldest son raises his voice against me that means he's had it with me and is handing me over to his younger brother. They rush to bring me to the outer limits of life, beyond which there is nothing. It is not my death that they are intent upon, just my reaching death completely empty, a shell devoid of anything but my corpse. They scold me for being retarded and unable to keep up with their estimations of my advanced age. They increase my age by months and years, and then say that I'm not acting my age. As if I am denying my advanced age to trick them or to prove the claim I made to my son's wife, that 'the Angel of Death, Azraa'eel, has no power over me'.

It is not simply my voice that reminds them of my shameful refusal to act my age, but my whole appearance. They wonder why I hold my head up like that when I look at one of them, why my legs are so long, why my hand moves the cane forward the way it does. They take the extra bones in my feet as another sign of my strength, the strength that they insist should be dwindling. They want my body to become delicate and frail, to stay ill, for my skin to become thin, red, and brittle, like the skin of old people who have alternated over a long time between long hours of sleeping and illness.

Yes. I have decided. I definitely won't tell my son when he comes – he wouldn't say anything to them anyway. They will bring him into their gathering the minute he arrives, and sit him down on a chair in their midst, showing him the way as if he was blind. He'll spend his time silently looking on, and anyway their lady guest isn't going to quit talking because she figures that she is exchanging her talk for their clean air and their food. They will continue to cling about her, asking her questions so they can laugh at her responses. They turn their faces towards her, faces made white and round from so much washing and eating. 'Like moons', their mother says, pleased to see their cheeks dangling like loose bellies. No, he won't say anything to them and he'll just go silently to the table laden with food. His wife will move a plate closer to him and tell him to eat, her mouth so full of food it's difficult to swallow.

The party continues non-stop. My son sees this as proof of their cleverness, and so finishes his food silently, and is the first to return to his chair. Like me, he is not good when it comes to talking, doesn't know how to come and go or wander about in it. My cousin Hajj Youssef always spoke in the long-winded manner of the town sheikhs, saying very little in a circular, tedious way. I used to think he was trying to cozy up or make amends to men he once chided and rebuked, so I would become agitated sitting there, and not know what to do. I once felt like kicking a beggar who didn't like what I had given him, but he took hold of me and started reciting verses from the Qur'an. My son moves away from the table because he can't keep up with their laughter. He can't stay with the pace of the performance of the laughing woman. She is so used to being a guest in people's houses that in an instant she can change her manner, put on different faces, and mimic different voices.

Their faces are round and white, so much do they eat and wash. I still can take on the entire house from one end to the other with my voice raised at their children, or calling out for one of them to pass by my window, or complaining about their mother to their father, or making noises on my *mastaba* to keep them wary of me. I hold sway over the whole house to stoke my irritation and remind them of it. I tell Ahmad to get away from my window, so that he will go tell them: 'He drove me away from his window.' I do this to keep them from getting accustomed to living their lives as if I were not present here underneath them. When I raise my voice against the children, I want everyone upstairs to hear and I want them to get into some kind of commotion regarding me. Their mother is going to say, with them all lined up on the balcony looking over at me, that she will never rest easy in the house until I die. I begin to boil with rage all over again, because it only takes two days of me being silent and secluded for my son to get used to not being worried about me. Just two days, after which it will be hard for me to continue desiring whatever it is I had wanted. At that point, I too can stop worrying about myself and just stay in my bed, with my son bringing me food. But I'd prefer to sleep instead.

Their bodies share the same pallor, which their mother calls cleanliness, without shrinking away from the stench of decay that is at the heart of their paleness. The eldest brought a slice of pear up to my mouth with fingers scraped clean, leaving traces of dead and scaling skin. I brought my mouth forward to snatch it up just the way a bird does to peck at a grain to eat, snatching it cleanly away from all surrounding entrapments. They call it 'cleanliness' for the palms of one's hands to stay tender with the dampness and moisture exuding from them. But one has to get one's hands dirty to require cleaning, and to grab onto things that are dry and rough. He ought to clean his hands with dirt and not with the pear which will only make them more slippery and smelly.

I didn't say anything to Ahmad's father when he arrived holding his plate of food out in front of him. He appeared tired, his tall and lean body swaying a little from being so late getting back from work. I said to him, 'Dinner time has passed, Father, this is no time to eat.' He asked me if I would like him to make some tea. I climbed up into my bed as he stood in the middle of the room. I knew he would feel sorry for me, thinking that I was taking to my bed out of feebleness, not because I might be feeling sleepy. He approached to cover me, but I said, 'Sit down a little, they are going to be enjoying their evening upstairs, so don't worry about them.' He didn't take a seat. He has become accustomed to keeping his visits short, and he makes them shorter each time. He doesn't seem to want to go upstairs; he seems to be brooding about something.

Still, he doesn't sit down; there is little talk between us, to the point that I wouldn't know what to talk about if he did sit down. When I used to ask him about his work he would just praise and thank God, thinking that I would never understand anything that he might have to say. And he doesn't tell them anything about it upstairs, either. He gets up from the table after he has eaten and moves off to the remote chair at the other end of the balcony. He doesn't converse with them, and I can't attract him towards me, for how could I ever go about starting the kind of conversation with him that enables two people to renew their companionship? They are preoccupied with their evening enjoyment and he is at a loss for what to do. 'Sit down, son', I say, knowing that still doesn't mean he'll talk to me. He'll spend the time in mute silence, and I'll end up wanting him to go, just to lighten the embarrassment produced by our silence. He will get up after a short while and stand opposite me on the verge of saying: 'There, I've sat down and we haven't done anything.' I'll think of something to say as he steps towards the door; I'll tell him to take the plate with him, tell his brother to come see me, leave the door open, and be careful going up the stairs in the darkness. I talk a lot to him during his exit so that he will forget the silence that was there between us, and to have him understand that the next time he comes by we will talk a lot, in this way.

I can't strike up a companionship with him if I don't know what to discuss with him. 'How is your health coming along?' he asks, and I mumble some of the things people say when asked about their health. He doesn't do any better when I ask him about his work. He's not a talker, though his family fritters away the time in meaningless conversation day in and day out. There is nothing wrong with not talking, I don't like it either, but he doesn't understand that it is possible for a father and son to sit like this together without talking. I am so bothered with his embarrassment that during those few minutes he spends with me I want him to leave.

I can hardly find it in me to let go and relax in his presence, let alone allow some blissful elderly contentment to flow through my being and put me to sleep. It is as if I am lying on the bed with him on the sofa near me, and each one of us is looking off at wherever suits us. He'll be thinking of his business, although he will distract himself with his palms and squeeze them together and pull them apart like a child. We spend a long time together in silence like this, with neither of us talking about anything other than what pops randomly into our heads. For instance, he'll ask me who that wide tract of land belongs to, since he was thinking about it as he was flipping his hands around in front of him. I'm not irritated that he doesn't hear me when I reply, because I myself hesitate in replying, and I too am very slow. And because I know he asked that question unintentionally, as if it rose up of its own accord and without disrupting his state of abandonment to his thoughts.

We sit close to one another like this without the need to talk. He doesn't understand this silence; he thinks people only meet one another for a purpose, and go on their separate ways when it's achieved. He places the plate of food in front of me and tidies up my things and asks me: 'How is your health, Father?' And then he shifts about, getting ready to leave. He implements everything in a short time, as if he was a janitor who had popped into my room while going on his rounds down the hall.

He interprets our silence as an inability to speak, and thinks that we must take leave of one another because we've fallen silent. And I can't say for sure that our lack of conversation is because there is no need for it, or that it necessarily gives me pleasure to sit in silence.

Companionship between fathers and their sons is one of those things that is not announced or pointed out. It is even too much to tell him: 'I've missed you, son.' That could land us in state of confusion that we couldn't manage. He'd freeze in his place, aghast, and then look around for a way out as if I had betrayed a confidence.

So when he comes in I'll ask him: 'Why do you folks leave me alone like this?' It must appear to be mildly scolding so that each of us can play his appropriate role. He'll put the plate of food on the little table and begin to straighten up my things and sweep my room, and I'll get heavily out of bed without a word, because someone has told me it's time to eat.

If I had told him about what happened, the yelling on the steps, the feigned stroke, the feeding of the pears on the balcony, he would think I was dragging him into an argument that he would lose. Not because they were in the right, but because of their sheer numbers. They would surge to answer him in a hysterical mass. His wife would go back over events in which I would be the one who raised his voice or lifted an angry hand. Ahmad would say I was not ill, but just put on an act to scare them. Their elder son would plunge into a detailed analysis of my problems and my entire life, and say that I behave the way I do because of loneliness and boredom.

They would continue to exchange their arguments between themselves even after he'd surrendered into silence. They would modulate their opinions of me according to the tenor of the discussion, its peaks and valleys. They would reach a consensus on my loneliness and boredom, but then reverse when their mother reminded them of my haughtiness and cruel streak. Later, perhaps, they'd even take a turn at pitying me, attempting to please my son who would've isolated himself in the corner, propping his head on his hands.

They won't be able to drop the subject of my behavior until the laughing lady amuses them with another impression or ridiculous question, and then they'll laugh and wait for her to do another. She'll start from the last thing that was said, then lead away from it as if dragging a donkey by its halter. She knows they won't be able to stop or shift direction. They won't tolerate any silence, but they will allow another round of talk to *allow* them to forget what they were just talking about. I myself will behave as if I hadn't heard Ahmad's shrill laughter and the uproar it provoked. And perhaps I will go up to their house tomorrow to start off where the session with the pear had ended. I'll go up to their house and head for the same chair, not only so I can forget what they said, but also to help them forget. In this way I get to choose the most suitable portrait of myself, among the ones they've painted. I will spend the evening with them, taking on the aspect of someone who is bored and lonely. I won't cast my gaze far off, but will keep my eyes on things close by to me, as if defining the limits of my realm. I won't speak to anyone who is not nearby, and then it'll be only two or three words, after which I will go back into my silence. In any case I won't sit for long; if I overstay they'll weave a web of talk that they'll use to snare and slander me.

The next day, I go upstairs. The eldest grandson hands me over to his younger brother, the one with the 100-pound haircut. The whole family is lined up on the balcony, and the children are gathered at the end of the *dar* near the water basins. He begins to shout at me again, along the same lines as yesterday. I take it silently since I won't be able to come up with anything new, after claiming to have had a stroke yesterday. I won't be able to remind him of our living together in the house and my preparing his meals for him with my own hands. He won't respond to my silence, and will himself, like me, not go too far, as long as they are all lined up there behind him on the balcony. But he will finish off his shouting at me, the shouting he couldn't finish yesterday because of my 'stroke'. It *is* his turn, after his brother's earlier in the day, yesterday, and he has, after all, to set an example for his youngest brother, Ahmad, who is preparing for his round with me by playing under my window, and knocking on the wooden table with the bones of his hand.

IX

I started to cry when my grandson asked me why I didn't shave my beard. Not so he'd understand that no one takes me to Nabatiyah, but to convey my dismay at my two sons who haven't stopped reprimanding me from the moment they came in to me. I was sitting on the edge of my bed, passing my hand along the surface of the bedding as if I was smoothing and straightening it out. The two of them can't seem to tolerate anything today. Abu Fayez told me that the doctors have other work to attend to besides me, when I told him to fetch one. When I put my hand on my heart in pain, he asked me if I was expecting not to have any aches at 100 years old. When I lifted my hand for them to help me stand up, they did not act kindly or gently, but treated me like they were grabbing a stranger. They asked me, 'Where to?', and I nodded my head towards the *mastaba*. 'He pisses out there, on the *mastaba*', he said to his brother, pulling a disgusted face with his mouth and tongue.

My grandson retreated to the farthest end of the room, and the two of them stayed standing where they were. My crying came up spontaneously, and I didn't embellish it for extra effect. It was like the crying of a man crying alone. My hand didn't lift off of the bedspread, my head didn't tremble, and my eyes stayed fixed looking on the ground in front of me. The two of them stayed standing where they were, and my grandson withdrew to the furthest corner of the room, seeking to save himself from the constricting and oppressive situation into which I had placed them all. My two sons didn't know what to do. It was as if, by crying, I had revealed that I fully understood the meaning of the words directed at me, and the severity and harshness underneath. It appeared to them that I remained in full possession of this awareness, and that I was only now openly revealing this to them, my patience worn thin and no longer able to keep up the masquerade they wanted me to play.

My crying was real, of the kind that you cannot add words to but that overcomes you and that you make an effort to bring to an end. They didn't come towards me and they didn't step back. I knew they were alarmed at this withdrawal, my obliviousness of them. It was as if they saw an angel that had come to warn them of a punishment for their treatment of me. I stood up by myself, with my hand on the edge of the bed for support. With the other hand I began to pull down the blanket to get into bed. I appeared, once I was lying down, to be expelling them from the room, having turned my face towards the wall. I heard them asking my grandson, still in the farthest end of the room, why he had chosen this moment to remind me about my ragged beard. Abu Fayez whispered these words, but it was as if he spat them from his turned-up, sneering lips. I knew he was trying to dispel his anxiousness by returning matters to their previous state, in which my tears always appeared to be a combination of whining, trickery, and feeble-mindedness. His rebuke of his nephew had a quick effect on me, such that I felt that the roles we had been playing had suddenly vanished, and that I was losing the strength I had been able to garner from true crying and from withdrawing into myself.

I told the two of them, as they were slipping outdoors, to bring Sayyid Mahdi to me from his town. They stood a while at the door, peering at my face as though they were trying to see if there was anything there they might recognize. I had decided to leave a request for Sayyid Mahdi for a more urgent and desperate time, because they only respond once to any request or need of mine. One time the doctor came, and went about quickly examining me and talking to me about my eating and my sleeping as if he was talking to a small child. One time they believed that I'd had a stroke, and brought me upstairs to their home and spent the evening with me under their watch. One time my crying caused them concern and bewilderment, but after that if I cry they will say that I liked playing that role so well that I want to play it every time I meet them. Any particular thing will bring a benefit on one occasion only. I tell my son Qassem to sit down, yet I know that he won't do it because the words don't come forth as strongly as they did on the first occasion that I used them. I used them hesitantly the second time, they came out as echoes of previous sounds.

'I want a doctor, Abu Fayez', I said, but he replies that the doctors have a lot of work to do besides dealing with me. They don't listen to me even when I am pointing out with my hands the places that give me pain, because they believe that pain can be nothing new for me. They want me to become more skilled in manifesting my pain so that they can believe me, or find ways of convincing them that I really need a doctor. I have to invent new methods and compose new tricks to say what I want to say. This has to appear to be true and real, as long as they hold fast to their belief that I am full of trickery and invention. But when I told the two of them to bring Sayyid Mahdi, I knew they'd bring him. Not only because it is the first time I'd asked for him, but because it signaled to them that I was giving into my death and accepting it. The two of them looked me over to search for some indication that they would recognize. I kept up the same demeanor, as it is not befitting for someone anticipating death to soften his voice and change his appearance. I am taking my revenge on them for pushing me towards death. They both came up to me and Abu Fayez asked me what I was feeling. So I said: 'She is coming out.'

'How?' he asked. I gestured towards my heart then spat a clump of spit out of my mouth as if I was expelling air and steam that had been surrounding and blocking it. The two of them went out in a hurry leaving me with my grandson; he abandons his position at the far end of the room and approaches me to ask if I need anything, then he says he is going out and will come back soon. Alone in the room I waited for Sayyid Mahdi, with whom I will not be permitted to speak or be on my own. He won't ask me where I am feeling the pain; the boys will have already told him in the car. He'll ascertain that I've given up on life. The two of them will do all the talking needed before they get to my door. They will meet despite their differences with regard to me, and Sayyid Mahdi will choose to be closer to their ages, and he won't spend much time going back and forth in conversation with me. He'll even say what they want him to say, and he will greet them the way older people typically greet those who are younger than them.

But no, he didn't. He raced ahead of them in his turban and with the sides of his cloak flying out behind him, and they were unable to keep up with him through the courtyard and were befuddled by his swiftness and his commanding demeanor. He told them to remain outside the room when they tried to come in behind him. I stirred to get up out of bed for him, but, using two swift movements of his hand, he instructed me to remain lying stretched out. I said *salaam 'alaykom* to him as he came up to me, simultaneously searching for a chair to put next to my bed. He returned the greeting, "*Alaykom as-salaam*, and the blessings of God', as he picked up the chair he found at the far end of the room. He brought it right up against the bed and sat down, repeating once more his salutation as if he was starting his arrival all over again.

I said to him: 'It's a most vile and despicable life, Sayyid Mahdi.' I put on an act of crying so that he wouldn't take what I said to mean that I am doing it in my bed. He recited a verse or two of the Qur'an saying that God is with those who are patient. He then turned to occupy himself with his rosary, waiting for me to end my crying. I asked him: 'Did your father cry in his last days?' He recited another verse from the Qur'an, without taking his eyes off the rosary in his hands. He kept silent with his head bowed low, waiting for me to start talking the talk for which I'd summoned him. 'They are treating me badly', I said, matter-of-factly, devoid of any complaining. He lifted his eyes towards me and thought a little before asking me if they were leaving me alone in my illness. I told him they are letting their children shout and yell at me, and allowing them to insult me. I almost started crying again, but then saw his wide, questioning eyes, as if he was expecting me to tell him that they were beating me.

'And food?' he asked. 'Are they stingy with it?'

'I'm not eating the way they do – just one plate, Sayyid Mahdi, the way they feed dogs and cats. And they stand around on top of me until I eat it and then they take it away with them.'

'But is it enough for you, what you are getting?'

'It's not edible, Sayyid Mahdi, it's cold and there is no broth or gravy in any of it.'

'Well, do they bring it on time?'

'On time and before it's time. They bring lunch before noontime to get it over with early. Tell me, Sayyid Mahdi, did your father know much about death when he was on his deathbed?'

There was no response so I asked another question: 'What do I do with them, Sayyid Mahdi? Is there anything I can do?'

'Do you intend to forgive them and give them your blessing?'

It was my turn not to answer. I knew he would go see them

right after leaving me and convey what would be, if I told the truth, effectively my curse against them.

He repeated his question.

I looked away, not wanting to lie to Sayyid Mahdi.

He tried a different approach. 'So, you forgive them, then?'

Again, I turned my head aside and said nothing. We sat silently for a moment then I glanced at him in a friendly way to remind him of the old conversations we used to have.

'I want them to obey me, Sayyid Mahdi', I said. He looked at me wryly, obviously contemplating asking me if I still planned for a future.

'I don't mean that they have to live according to my dictate, just that they obey me regarding what concerns me.'

He made a face that inferred he thought I'd only sent after him to complain about my children.

'Where is your illness?' he asked.

'In my heart, and in my age too', I said, gesturing with my hand to the distance between my feet and head, indicating that everything gave me pain.

He nodded.

'Once,' I began, 'there was a lot of power in this body of mine but they have killed it. They have destroyed my body, Sayyid Mahdi, destroyed it with abandonment, insult, and renunciation. They have made me swallow their insults so that I go to sleep wide awake, ashamed that my body is stronger than my age. And I kill it off along with them by sitting, sleeping, and waiting for death. They evicted me from my bakery and from my land, and they have occupied my house with their children. They accuse me of being feeble and senile as if they want me to fall into being that way. They want me to hurry up and reach 100 because they think no one lives beyond that. They have prohibited me from having any desire, they have tried to stamp it out as if it was a snake slithering into their houses.'

I paid no heed to my voice, which got louder and louder until it reached the two of them out there on the *mastaba*. They both heard me. They even cracked open the door to hurry things up and bring the conversation to an end. Sayyid Mahdi scolded them, saying we weren't done yet, so they retreated from the door and shut it again.

'Should I say anything to them?' he asked in the tone one uses to end a conversation.

'We haven't spoken about anything yet', I said.

'What should we talk about?'

'About my will.'

'Say it, then ... say it.'

He landed me into silence again. I could tell he wanted me to say things he could pass on to them upstairs. I tried to collect my thoughts, get my wits about me. I had forgotten who I'd given the 10,000 pounds to for safekeeping.

'Do you owe anybody anything, any debts?' he asked.

'Nothing, except that my wife Hajja Khadija's sister Fatima never forgave me.'

'And have you forgiven her for not forgiving you?' he asked.

'I left the room angry after I asked her twice to forgive me without her answering me. I didn't know that she understood my scolding her and yelling at her. She would just move along when I would push her with my hands, she never said a thing to anybody about it.'

'Who apart from her?'

'I didn't ask anyone. I didn't even ask my wife', I said.

He smiled, shook his head. 'I mean, are you in debt to anyone besides her, do you owe anybody any money?'

'They have taken all of the money, all of my wealth. I bequeathed it to them while still alive, Sayyid Mahdi.'

'And the house?'

'It's theirs too. I am living in their house.'

'So what will you say in your last will and testament?'

I hadn't realized that I had nothing to say to him. I understood then that I truly had nothing, I'd given it all away. There was nothing to bequeath. They already had it. Maybe I shouldn't have sent after him ...

'Nothing, Sayyid Mahdi, nothing.'

'Have you forgotten something, anything you haven't said?'

'Nothing.'

He got up, straightened his cloak about his shoulders, recited another verse from the Qur'an exhorting me to be patient, and then turned towards the door which my two sons opened as he approached. In the doorway, he turned and asked where I wanted to be buried.

'In the cemetery, Sayyid Mahdi, in the cemetery', I said.

X

There are a lot of people in Muhammad Habib's house, some of them I know and others I don't. They fill the room into which chairs, couches, and large cushions – some of them from my house – have been placed. The light in the room comes from the Lux kerosene lantern they've suspended out-side. The appearance of Muhammad Habib's face fluctuates between youth and old age. When he leans in one particular direction, he looks twenty or thirty years younger. Not as he actually looked in those days, but with skin unnaturally taut and rosy. His normal appearance, the age I know him as, returns as he moves away from me, and I see him from another angle. I forget to ask why he doesn't bring the Lux lantern inside. The room grows darker. Muhammad Habib is at the other end. I consider getting the Lux lantern, sus-pended from the tree outside, but discover that I don't have the strength to move. It is obvious everyone plans to spend their evening in this room, which gives off an ancient smell that suits this gathering. Among the men I know in the crowd there are some ancient ones. I only just learned that they are relatives of Muhammad Habib.

Heavy and stuck in my seat, I can't raise my hand to signal to Muhammad Habib. But he senses what is going on with me and flies to my side. His face changes again: even more rosy and unnatural. He greets me with successive movements of his hand from his head to his belly as if he is decorating himself. I think that perhaps he is inviting me to make fun of him, but his fixed gaze and artificial-looking face make me feel uneasy. So I smile at him and my smile makes my face look stiff, because it makes it lengthen so much.

Some faces I know and others I don't. In any case, I feel alone among them. They all seem to have been partying for some time together before I turned up. They had sent two men for me. They knocked on my door until I got up. I shouldn't have come along with them, but they were at my door shouting and I knew they would carry on all evening if I were to shut the door in their faces. I was so determined to quiet them, I left without my slippers. They showed me to Muhammad Habib's house, and then went to bring other men from their houses to the gathering. So here I am alone in my bare feet in the party, while Muhammad Habib wears his copious, swirling, and crisply ironed wraps.

They sit, smoke, and talk to one another, some of them sitting in my chairs. I have no idea how my furniture ended up at Muhammad Habib's house. I do not remember anyone coming for it. Muhammad Habib disappears for a while and my sense of loneliness intensifies. When he returns carrying a tray of tea glasses, I am overjoyed to see him. Muhammad Habib leans over, presenting the tea tray and then pulling it away as a joke. The other men laugh. He does this a few times.

I laugh too, but, again, when I get close to his face, it frightens me. It's like he's threatening me for once making fun of him. He leaves with the tray before I can take a glass from it.

I thought as I got out of my bed that I was heading for their outhouse, the one under the tree where the Lux lantern hangs. I find my way to a bucket and I pee into it. I am still bothered by the looks from Muhammad Habib which grew more menacing the closer he got to me. I peed in haste but without spilling any drops on my clothes, and I tossed the contents of the bucket, in a quick movement so no one would see me, onto the terrace. I returned the bucket to its place and headed back to my bed in a hurry, afraid that they would send the men to come get me and try to haul me back to the party.

But somehow I ended up back at the party anyway. The crowd had thinned out and Muhammad Habib apologized for taking away the tea tray before I'd had a chance to grab a glass. He shook his head to let me know he would bring some real tea around for me. His wife sat on a large carpet cushion not far from me. I was surprised because I thought she had died. When Muhammad Habib turned his back to us she gave me a look and her eyes darted to her husband. She smiled, revealing that she too thought him strange, even ridiculous in his old-style clothing, dancing around, his face rosy and unnaturally taut. Her eyes shone brightly in her shriveled and wrinkled face. Her eyebrows were plucked and stretched as if they belonged to a woman of thirty. Muhammad Habib kept his back to me, perhaps in order for the woman's eyes to grow ever brighter and for them to come to an agreement with me about more than Muhammad Habib's clothes and motions.

But I felt repulsed by the wrinkled face which looked strange and scary around the bright shining eyes. Muhammad Habib moved out of the way to allow a throng of children to get by. They ran to me and starting stepping on my bare feet. One child after another took turns like it was a competition to see who could get rid of the extra bones in my feet.

My feet burned with pain, but amazingly I sat calmly while they hammered away on them with their hard little heels. However, when I put them on the ground with my weight upon them, in an effort to go, once again, to the *mastaba*, the pain shot through my body. They were swollen from the bruising, so I put all of my weight onto my cane and went off limping and swaying as best I could. The bucket was still in its place. It let off a strong odor when I lifted it, as if I had brought it to life by touching and lifting it from its place. The stench also emanated from the concrete gap underneath the *mastaba*, and from the side of the terrace on which I pitched the urine from my bucket. It was a powerful, penetrating smell, made up of many things, not just urine. I thought for a moment they must be pitching the piss from their buckets upstairs onto the terrace below. But then I remembered that urine only smells bad sometime after it has left our bodies. I almost fell over when I brought the bucket close to me, and came to realize that I would not be able to pee by myself anymore if my feet would not hold me up. I knew I couldn't prop myself up on the *mastaba* railing, with my hand needed for the cane and bucket. I'll sit, I thought, on one of the stairs.

The swelling had increased by the time I crawled, literally on my hands and knees, back into bed. I covered myself with the blanket, but I kept my head raised, so I wouldn't fall asleep again and risk having my feet trampled on by the children. I tucked the blanket under my feet to hide them from those terrors. An image of Muhammad Habib standing at the entrance to his house flashed before my eyes. I greeted him with the standard salutation of peace, and he smiled and bowed, moving his hand between his stomach and forehead. He repeated the movement and was about to do so again when I realized that I was falling asleep. I shook the drowsiness out of my head. I saw a light had started to come up outside, less bright than the lamp lit in my room, but it nevertheless had the power to attract me to it. I leaned my body towards the window and gave into a deep pre-dawn sleep.

I stared for a long time into the face of the person who had woken me up before I recognized him as my son. He carried a tray in one hand, and helped me sit up with the other. He asked me what was wrong. I looked inquisitively at him, as if I had been distracted and lost in thought. Realizing he couldn't get me out of bed with only one hand, he hesitated, not knowing where to place the tray. I gingerly pulled the blanket from my feet and then tried to lift the right one, then the left one. No use, they were simply dead weight.

'What's wrong with them?' my son asked.

They glowed, pink and swollen. I kept silent so as not to dispel the entire evening's anxieties with a quick answer.

'What's wrong with them?', he asked again, leaning over for a closer look.

I didn't reply this time either. Sharp pain flashed across my face as I got ready to stand on them.

'Why are they so swollen like this?' my son asked, trying to move me from my bed to the couch nearby. I cowered, pulled away from him and nestled deep into the bed. There was a flash of recognition on his face; it had obviously dawned on him that I couldn't stand up.

When he asked me if I would eat, I shook my head in refusal.

'They put steel into the tips of their shoes', I said.

'Who does, Father?'

'They do. The kids in Muhammad Habib's house.'

He studied my face, taking in my demeanor, looking for clues. 'And where did you see them, Father?', he asked.

'Who are you talking about?'

'The kids in Muhammad Habib's house.'

I raised my feet off the ground for him to examine.

'What should I do about them?' I asked. 'Will you get me the doctor from Nabatiyah?'

'I'll be back, Father. I'll be back, but if you need anything tap on the window with your cane.'

Not much time passed before the grandchildren trickled down from the balcony to see for themselves. The eldest one delicately probed my feet with the tips of his fingers, using the same deliberateness he did when popping the pear slices into my mouth. He asked, in an innocent voice, what was wrong with them. I told him they were swollen.

His brother came next. His movements alternated between impetuousness and curiosity, and he could not conceal his skepticism based on everything he'd heard about me. He was about to speak, but his brother silenced him. As for their sister, she stood near to the door and asked how I felt – the water pail and cleaning implements in her hands, to wash my piss off the stairs. She made a point of displaying them prominently so I could see.

There had obviously been a discussion upstairs about my senility and they were the scouting party, sent down to investigate and confirm the state I was in, each one doing so in his or her own way. She stood in front of me with her pail and brushes in hand. She must've figured that someone who pisses on the stairs is not going to be shocked by her sweeping and washing away the traces.

She asked, once again, since I apparently didn't answer the first time, 'How is your health, grandpa?'

Again, I kept quiet. I shifted my head from one to the other. The older one asked when the pain started, looking at my feet from every angle. Ahmad treats it as an inquisition, wanting to know exactly why this happened, so he can cross-examine what I say versus what his father said I'd claimed earlier. They try to get me to reveal more evidence of my condition. They want me to say something, it is somehow not sufficient to see my urine on their stairs or my slips of the tongue in front of their father, which he so adeptly conveys to them.

He must have told them I'd gone senile. 'He has gone senile, and that's all there is to it,' he probably told them, and their inquisitiveness and nosiness increased.

'What has he done?' they probably asked.

'What did he do?' the girl probably asked.

'What did he say?' Ahmad no doubt inquired.

They all want the same story, and they want the entire story not just a summary, or punch line – the kids in Muhammad Habib's house who put steel into the tips of their shoes to crush my feet. They need to confirm my debility, see what my face looks like after the pain and confusion has wracked it.

'I am going to the stairs', the girl said, hoisting the pail up high for all to see.

'To the stairs? Be careful you don't fall', Ahmad said in a high-pitched voice.

'Go ahead, go ahead', her older brother said, then asked me: 'Do they hurt a lot, grandpa?'

I raised my feet off the ground to show just how much the pain diminishes and shrinks my face, and how it takes hold of it.

'Why don't they bring me a doctor from Nabatiyah?' I ask.

He crouches next to my feet, scanning them for something he'd missed earlier. 'We'll wait until dusk', he said.

The two of them didn't do anything for me. They left me alone where they found me.

I know upstairs they are reporting their findings. I can see Ahmad standing there as he tells them what he and his brothers said, and how his sister lifted the pail high for me to see. The kids will laugh at their own jokes, compensating for having returned empty-handed. They will rework their interpretations based on my reputation and my demeanor, in order to unearth sure signs of my senility. Not just from my sidelong glances and stares but from the swelling that turns my feet bloated and enormous.

'This kind of thing only happens to people when their

minds have lost the ability to manage their bodies', the eldest grandson, who relished poking the swelling with his fingers, will tell his parents. He sees this as a sign of how things with me are getting out of control, with all the freak occurrences, sudden twists and turns taking place, things that illnesses normally don't entail.

Later, the eldest will look at my face and ask what's wrong, pointing to the whiteness spreading over my eyes. He thinks this doesn't only affect my vision, but also my senses, causing me to forget things I knew, and to lose track of myself. But he doesn't ask 'What's wrong with your eyes, grandpa?' Because he thinks it's a secret only he knows.

They see I've decayed from inside and outside at the same time, that I am afflicted by those things that change color with age. Their sister looks for eggs in my urine because she thinks it is not possible for something to emerge from my body that has not been corrupted and spoilt by my age. She continues to scrub the urine from the stairway but is careful not to submerge the broom in it, and she uses an abundance of water as if she is trying to drown the impurity.

Abu Fayez won't ask me, when he next comes around, why I pissed on the stairwell, but he will put on his disgusted and frowning face, with his nose and lips scrunched and turned up to ward off the terrible odor.

'Do you see', he will all but ask me, 'wouldn't it have been better for you to die of your last illness?' Then he will look at my glowing, pulsating feet.

He will not ask about pissing on the stairs because my alleged senility preserves me from any blame for this. They won't go back to yelling down at me in the courtyard of the *dar*, but they will now stand close by to me, waiting to hear what I have to say. I won't be angry with them, and they won't be angry with me.

Where is the doctor? They'll say that he is on his way. He got delayed by an accident, Ahmad will say. He is waiting at this moment for another car to bring him, since his car was totaled, he'll claim. Then, upstairs, he'll shriek with laughter at his elaborate story and how easy I am to put off now.

As for his father, he will see my pee on the stairs and not say anything either. But he won't say anything ever again to me when he enters my room, because he thinks that I am no longer in possession of my faculties. He'll wait for his brother to ask him what they should do about my stench. They will discuss this right in front of me, and I will hear everything but keep silent, as I know that I must pay the price for their pretending not to notice my misdeeds, and for their ceasing to scold me for every little thing. I will have to convince them every time that I am still oblivious to everything around me. Otherwise they will eventually ask, 'So, why did you piss on the stairs?' And they will lecture me about using the bucket. At that point I'll raise my voice in anger: 'And where do you want me to do it? Isn't it enough that I have hide and bury my shit like a cat?'

I'll give them one of these remarks whenever I see that their patience is wearing thin. They left me alone with swollen feet, unable to get up. I grabbed my cane and started to pound with it against the window. They were upstairs and must have been waiting for the sound, because no sooner had I put my cane down than I heard them galloping down the stairs. They probably thought I would come clean and admit that I'd orchestrated all this, damaged my own feet to get their attention. But it was just Ahmad alone.

'What do you want, granddad?'

'My food. I want my food. Do your parents think that people can live without eating?'

It won't take long for my remark to get back to them all upstairs. He will tell them: 'My food, I want my food ...', and he will complete the account of what I said about them.

They'll ask again, 'What did he say?'

He will repeat, 'My food, I want my food ...', using my accent.

'And how did he say it?' they'll ask.

His mother will say that my senility is only going to make me nastier and more violent, and she'll tell her daughter not to fill my plate too much or my stomach might burst and despoil everything.

'Is this how you people eat?' I say when he brings the plate.

He knows I am trying to pick a fight with him. He stops, befuddled, in front of me, and says nothing, afraid of what I might do.

'Eat, grandpa, eat,' he finally says.

'And where is your father?'

'Eat, grandpa,' he says, retreating towards the door, wary I may knock something over with my cane to block his exit.

When they came together at dusk, I told them not to leave me alone in the night. Abu Fayez looked at me from a distance of a few paces, and asked his brother if I really had not eaten all day.

'He asks for food that he doesn't eat.'

I shift my gaze between the two of them, waiting for them to make a decision.

'Do they give you pain?' Abu Fayez asks.

I fix my eyes on him.

'Your feet, do they give you pain?'

I gesture with my hand lightly for him to repeat his question, which I didn't understand.

He returned to where he had been standing before, near his brother, and then they both moved close to me as he asked: 'Should we bring you a doctor from Nabatiyah?'

I don't say anything. I know they'll talk about my silence later.

I muttered as they moved towards the door.

'What did you say?' Abu Fayez asks.

'Don't go out tonight.'

'Why not?'

'So they don't come and take me to Muhammad Habib's house!'

'Who do you mean, Father? Who are they?'

XI

My grandfather Sheikh Ahmad lifted himself up from his funeral bier as it was being carried and lowered into his tomb. There was a large mass of people gathered, and sometimes I was there walking among them, other times I sat waiting for them on top of a tall tombstone. There were so many people, climbing towards a large house decked out with banners and flags, that I forgot they were there to bury my grandfather.

The procession moved towards the cemetery when I started to hear their stomping. I could make out the banner of our hometown: it had unfurled despite the lack of wind and hung limply. Still, the verse of poetry inscribed on it was clearly visible. It was vibrant green, and above the calligraphic lettering that stretched across its entire width, there was the image of two fists grasping the handle of a single sword.

I knew that my grandfather was seeking me when he lifted himself out of his bier, although I busied myself with looking at all of the feet carrying him. But he returned once more and called out for me. He sat up and slid over to the side, apparently making room for me to squeeze in beside him. The two fists on the banner began to move the sword high and low, and a panic surged through me that the crowd, along with the bearers, might scatter, and my grandfather would fall to the ground, right out of his bier. Pandemonium had truly spread through the crowd, and my father's brothers had abandoned their positions, exchanging loud whispers amongst themselves, like they were making preparations for a battle in which many people would inevitably be killed. I could see them clearly from my vantage point on top of the tombstone. Frightened, I could not shake the awareness of the fact that I was not a young boy like I had been at his funeral, but that I was my current age, the old man I had been before I laid down to sleep.

The terror at the possible violence shook me from my sleep. I was in the same clothes from my dream, clothes which I'd never questioned in the dream as being inappropriate for attending my grandfather's funeral. They are the same thick striped pajamas with the frayed collar. I am entering and exiting dream worlds more easily than I can move from one room to another. There are no doors to open or shut.

I was all alone, the only old and grayed sheikh among them, as if I had never known any other body than the one I am now inhabiting. I remain as I am now in my dreams so I know I am at the end of my life. My appearance comes into my dream to carve my features deeply, as if someone were tracing with a thick pen to reinforce the faint lines of a quickly sketched picture. That is so that I should never forget that I am at this age, so that I should know what I am before I do anything or think about anything. I need to ask myself how I should be, how I should speak, now that I have gotten so close to 100 years old.

I said to Ahmad, 'How can you leave me alone when I am 100 years old?' I told him I would bring my own life to an end myself, seeing as the Angel of Death, Azraa'eel, apparently could do nothing for me. They were all gathered around me.

'How, granddad?'

'With an injection', I told him immediately, 'an injection like they gave to Hajja Amina to relieve her of her pain.'

'These are secrets, granddad, you shouldn't tell them,' their sister said with a laugh as everyone else turned their faces away because I had ruined their evening.

'Or I'll throw myself off your balcony.'

'Don't do it, don't do it grandpa. Don't put the blame on us', Ahmad said, playing the part, gearing up to prevent me.

'Sit down, sit down', the eldest one among them said, when he saw that I was about to cry.

'Goddamn this lifetime, it's too damn long', I said, 'no one in town ever got to this age.'

'No, grandpa, you're less than 100; you're also less than ninety.' He then explained how it is that I am not as old as I think.

When my son came by in the morning he found me holding on to the heater, stranded.

'What are you doing, Father?' he asked, lifting me by my armpits into bed. His hand held half a loaf of Arabic bread, rolled and wrapped up because he doubted that I would eat anything this time either. 'What's going on with you?' he asked as I started crying.

'Yesterday my grandfather Sheikh Ahmad died, and tomorrow I am going to catch up with him.'

He asked me if I had seen this in a dream, and I didn't answer him. I looked at him expecting him to repeat the question: 'Did you see your grandfather in a dream?' He did, and again, I didn't answer him. I kept gazing at him, disapproving of the way the words tumbled from his mouth. I dropped the crying face, as he adjusted the blanket and covered me up to my neck.

He told the people who came the day I got sick and stopped eating that my mind was sound but that the blood flow stops occasionally for just a few seconds. That's why I get scatter-brained and start talking about my dream world, he explained. He tapped his long index finger against his head to illustrate to them the artery in my head, and then he grasped it in the middle with two fingers from his other hand, to represent how the blood flow was stopped momentarily, then after a second he released the finger. They all stared at his fingers as they listened. In compensation for the death of his father he had an audience of five men, so he set about artfully embroidering what he was saying about me and my illness. No one interrupted him and no one asked him any questions.

'I am "so and so", do you recognize me?' Everyone says this upon entering my room, as they plop their face in front of mine and grab my limp hand, determined to shake it for me. I move my head a little to one side to indicate that I both recognize and welcome them. I move my head to the side very slightly, even less than someone asleep would do to get rid of a fly. It's because of my illness and my dizziness, my grandson will say to them, the depletion of energy from my body, or the emptiness of my diminished and constricted stomach, which he will demonstrate using compressed and contracted fingers.

'Do you recognize me, grandpa?' he asks. He is here with the others.

'You're Muhammad', I say.

'I'm not him, grandpa', he says, looking at me intently, giving me another guess. Their ages confuse me, so that I consider the old ones to be the young ones. It is as if they grew up without me knowing it. I'll call one by the name of his brother. In the same way, I mix up their family members, so that I give my youngest daughter a child that belongs to her sister.

'What's wrong with your hand, grandpa?'

'Nothing', I mumble, dropping it suddenly as if I had just been caught groping an exposed part of a woman's body. But I stare at my hand, examining its outline and the length of my fingernails, observing its similarities with my feet and their extra bones. I discover that I am still familiar with myself and can still sum up my appearance as it looked at various ages.

'Tell them to bring me a doctor from Nabatiyah.' I say this in a clipped tone, and don't repeat it a second time. Nor do I wait expectantly for him to leave and tell them, it's like the words just came out of me absent-mindedly.

'I want him to treat my pain, not my illness', I say, and lift my head up so they can see my face, diminished by pain.

'From where, grandpa?'

'From Nabatiyah!' I respond with anguish, so he'll do as I ask and not turn it into a joke.

'We'll get him, grandpa, hold on, we're coming.' He goes

out, taking one of them with him. They disappear for a short time, then return creating a commotion at the door: 'Come on in, Doctor, go right in.'

He steps between the two of them towards my exposed feet and begins to examine them without turning to see my face. He brings his eyes closer, turning them to his left, and holds them there. He mutters something in haste and returns to peering at my feet.

'It's a contemptible life,' I say, in a very formal tone, so they won't explode in laughter. They flee the room hastily, laughing at his antics in playing the role of the doctor. But they won't go beyond the *mastaba*. They will stay there rehashing the scene tens of times, and he will come along in the end acting like someone who has just this minute arrived.

'They are playing around with me', I say to my son. 'They all come and start laughing at me.'

'Who are you talking about, Father? Who are they?'

'Your children. Your children and your brothers' children. They ask me stuff so they can laugh at my answers; yesterday they brought in your sister's son and said he was a doctor.'

'And they laughed?' He asks the question with surprise and disapproval.

'Tell me, why are they in town, why have they come without their parents?'

'Did they laugh a lot?' He asks the question with a combative tone, a roar that rises in volume beyond anything that my small room can contain, with so little furnishings. It rumbles up powerful and reverberating, as if from out of the bottom of a huge pot, bouncing back and forth against its sides. He raises his voice like this in my defense, without knowing that I'm the only one he is frightening with it. I keep lying there very still, letting go of my body and letting my hand go limp, out of my fear that if I made any movement he would turn his anger upon me.

'A bunch of thugs', he says, 'them and their families.'

Later, upstairs, he announces that no one is allowed to enter this house that he doesn't approve of and who isn't going to do just what he says.

'Where is your mother?' I asked the one who had played the role of the doctor when he came by in the afternoon. He didn't reply. He stepped in the room and appeared irritated because he had arrived before the rest of them. He stuck to the window and began to look out at the tall gateway, whistling, afraid that his silence would get the better of him and that he wouldn't be able to keep them in stitches, by the time they arrived. I asked him again where his mother was, and again, he didn't answer.

'Where is your mom? Don't you understand me?'

He mumbled some faint noises, mouthing a few syllables from his lips, thinking that I would not hear, but that I would pretend to hear. He headed for the door.

I knew they had arrived from the smile on his face when he was halfway to the door. They came clamoring into the room, the strength of their bodies projecting forth myriad sounds with the clumping of their feet on the floor.

'How are you getting along, grandpa?' Ahmad asked, noting that the arteries in my head were pulsing away.

'Do you know who I am, grandpa?' one of them asked, raising his head from among the bunch.

'He's another doctor from Natabityah', Ahmad said when he saw me looking in the direction of the voice.

'Won't you eat, Father?'

I raised my eyes to look at him, hoping to eventually recognize him. He repeated it one more time, in a less strident voice, extending the rolled-up Arabic bread closer to my eyes. I thrust it away with my hand.

'You've got to eat, Father, you're going to die if you keep going like this without eating.'

I kept my eyes open, but unfocused, not looking at anything in their path, thinking about my body which my son sees to be feeble and lying in a heap under the blanket. I don't blink an eyelash and my hand, stuck on the pillow, doesn't move.

'Won't you eat, Father?', he asked again, lowering the bread to my eyes, which are vacant and unseeing.

'Father? Father ...'

I turned my face but kept my eyes blank as if they were looking at him blindly, this little movement intended to reassure him that I'm not dead yet.

I knew the whiteness clouding them made me look distant and befuddled, and that when I turned to him I must have appeared as if I couldn't single myself out from the circle of faces around us.

He became agitated with fear, and started looking like he was ready to flee the room, to escape the ghostly beings I was imagining and moving closer and closer to, all the time moving further from him.

He could see that I had begun my companionship with the dead, and that I had gone a long way from my body and my soul towards meeting them. He knew that whenever I wandered off or became absent I was facing death's direction. I kept straying towards it from the crossing I had come to, abandoning life, which was now back there, on the other side, and it wasn't strong enough to keep me on its side for very long. But when I dropped my head on the pillow and had my eyes fixed on him, he realized the dead folks were staying in their place to wait a bit more, just a bit more, until I returned.

XII

Those two don't stop laughing and saying filthy things, from the minute they turn up in the *dar*. They plod along slowly, sashaying past the high gateway and crossing the courtyard keeping a distance between them, looking around, like they planned to vandalize or deface it.

One of them plucks a rose from the little basin and ambles about sniffing it, as little girls would. She holds it in her rough and parched hand, and proffers it in the direction of her companion who is on the other side of the courtyard.

They mess about in the courtyard a bit more before they arrive at my place, acting like they'd entered a house where the inhabitants had all emigrated. They walk along my *mastaba*, stopping to converse, before one of them leans through my open window.

'He's awake.'

They weren't any more modest in their behavior when my son brought them in later to make my bed and clean my room.

'Where are your two sisters?' they asked him.

He bought himself some time by pretending to study me,

trying to think how he might answer them. The women began to joke around in front of me, despite his presence. He kept quiet, probably figuring I didn't understand the filthy things they were saying. The two of them became more daring in their jokes about me when he left. They came up to me boldly with wide eyes, pretending that the situation now permitted them to strip off my clothes and mess about with me.

They were both ugly. I was amazed that a man would marry both of them; the second wife didn't add much to whatever the first had. One of them pulled the blanket off me.

'Why don't you do it in the bathroom, granddad?' one of them asked.

I kept silent when they came closer to me, shaking their bodies in a little dance. I looked at the two of them as if I had no clue what was going on in front of me. It is going to be hard for them to clean up my body while my head is following their every move. Their husband would ban them from entering my room and washing me, if it appeared I liked watching them clean my genitals, because that would make him appear to be someone who hands his wife over to a stranger.

They dance about and say obscene things. I just empty my eyes and look into space, so that I can tolerate the possibility of seeing what they might come to see. And I won't ask my son if they behave that way when they are on the job at his work place, for that would be risking sounding like I am putting myself on a par with him, as if we were just two men having a discussion on an equal footing – whereas the reality is that I am fouling up my clothes and bedding with my own shit.

They act out roles in front of me, because they believe that one must be different from one's real self when in front of someone senile and feeble-minded. I am no less resourceful than they are. I change my appearance at will, clenching my teeth in pain, emptying my eyes of expression, and screaming from the core of my heart when they raise their voices and shout at me.

Neither of them is able to meet up with the real me unless it is when they put on their acts. The minute they talk among themselves they fall back into their original demeanors all over again, speaking in loud voices, thinking that I only can hear things said directly to me.

'Is he still able to get a hard-on?', one of the two women asked my son, as she glanced at her companion and then to me.

My son didn't answer her and he didn't answer me when I asked about his two sisters. He looked at me, obviously wondering what he should say. I didn't ask him again, since, if I did, he likely would say that someone who soils his bed doesn't have the right to choose his cleaner. He almost started to laugh with them when they acted like brides playing hard-to-get, trying not to enter the bedroom on their wedding night.

'What have you done to yourself?' The second woman asked the question after her mate had removed the blanket from me. The two of them looked disgusted at what they saw, and they abandoned their state of mirth. In order to keep them with me, I looked where they pointed.

They are two wicked ugly women. They are obscene and disgusted at the same time. They stare at my midsection searching for my genitals amid the filth.

'It has disappeared.' She said this to her companion who still stared at my crotch.

'Help me get him down to the floor, grab him from his shoulders', one of them said.

I looked at the place they planned to put me, as they carried me lightly in their hands, afraid they might drop me.

'On the straw mat, so his body doesn't get cold. Give me that pillow to put under his head', one of them said. They were strong. The second one kept holding me with one hand as she extended the other to reach the pillow. I could tell they were getting tired, though, but they held onto me and didn't let go. Realizing they were too tired to lower me to the mat, they decided to put me on the sofa instead.

'Put a sheet on top of the sofa, so he doesn't mess it up as well', one of them said.

I was feeble and light in their hands, and brittle-boned. I almost gestured to them to put me on the ground feet first, so that the one holding me by my shoulders would keep holding on to me.

'OK, let go of him, you first. Put his feet on the mat, on the straw mat.'

Their obscene manner came back to them the second they had me on the sofa.

They began pulling the sheets off the bed. Their butts moved about as they worked and they joked that they were invited to a wedding night with my shit. They had me face towards the bed so that I could see them and they could keep me involved in their foolery. The bed was completely fouled from end to end, so I knew a long time had passed without my being aware of it. My son, choking and with his voice breaking, asked, 'How did you manage all of that when you haven't eaten for a month?' But he didn't lift a finger. He kept me in my bed and left so that I couldn't ask him 'Where are your two sisters?' Because then he would start to curse them and say that they are 'taking in some air' and 'smelling the flowers' down in Beirut. To let me know that he is smelling something else right here in my room.

'Come here', one of the two said to the other as she held one end of the mattress. The other one gripped the opposite end.

'They've already flipped it before us', her companion said, panting. 'Should we get another one?'

The two looked at me, perhaps hoping I'd motion to where I stored the bedding. But I didn't do anything.

They looked around the room and noticed Hajja Khadija's bed through a gap in the door.

'Why don't you sleep over there?' the second one asked.

I averted my eyes to my bed. She gave me a long look, about to say something.

'Come on, work on this', said the other one, lifting her two hands high to reach the end of my bed. 'He doesn't want to sleep in a clean bed, he has gotten used to the smells. If he sleeps in that room he'll make it stink as well.'

My feet were raised high, the skin delicate and reddened. The area where the extra bones protruded was calloused and blistered. I was afraid they would see them and start to joke or hold them in their hands. I was also afraid of squeezing them down under the sofa, since they seemed too big and the women would know that I brought them down just to hide them.

'Why two women?' I had asked my son earlier when he hadn't answered my query about his two sisters. 'One would be enough.'

But I realized that their husband would not allow that either. He would compare that with a man and woman secluding themselves in a closed room, and he'd figure my lust would come back to me the minute I found myself stark naked and alone with one of his wives.

I wondered where they were going to wash me. Surely not on the sofa.

As if on cue, they started debating the issue: 'Should we clean him with cold water? Come on; let's clean him with cold water.'

They turned in my direction to find me staring hard at them like I didn't understand what they had said.

'Do you like cold water?' one of them asked.

I pretended I didn't understand. The two of them had finished making the bed. They came towards me suddenly, as if they had planned it all before and knew exactly what to do. I pulled my feet down from the edge of the sofa and shoved them into the cloth hanging on the edge.

'Show us your little pigeon now,' she said, as she was bending over my pajamas. Two together, to keep each other company, and so I won't be naked with just one of them. That's what their husband wants. For their part, they endured the sight of my excrement. That kind of shit doesn't come from food; it's the kind of filth expelled from a body so it's not taken to the next life.

'Show us your pecker,' she said, although she said it addressing her companion who was extending her thick and coarse hand, with its cracked skin, as if to grab something. He has intercourse with the two of them together in his home, and that way he no longer notices *her* parched and cracked hands, or *her* yellow teeth, because he is too busy flipping his eyes from one to the other and back, and trying to figure out their positions. He'll be looking at what one of them is doing with her hand, not at her hand. The two of them set about stripping me of my clothes from my waist down, but they hesitated and thought that I was about to make a mess on the sofa.

'We should have cleaned him on the bed,' said one, before her eyes landed on the straw mat.

'Raise him up by his shoulders,' she said, as her arms engulfed me from the middle of my thighs.

'Right here, here, where we put him the first time.'

They lowered me down where they'd put me the first time, then one of them ripped off my pajamas, pulling them from my knees. The two of them studied my crotch.

'It's disappeared,' said the one who had pulled the pajamas off me, as the other one went about searching for it in various places all the way up to my waist, as if looking for something misplaced. I extended my hand to hide it when she stretched her hand to grab it, and let out a cry when the hand dodged mine to get around me and grab it from another direction.

'He's worried about it,' she said to her mate, who was

still standing in her place. 'Go and get the water, give me the water,' she said, withdrawing a little and putting a hold on her obscene remarks until the other returned.

It was cold, and when they started splashing it on my thighs they both stopped talking as if they were waiting for me to yell out and scold them. I didn't say anything, though.

'Flip him over, so we can wash him from behind.' They wanted to wash away with water the remainder of the excrement that was sticking to me, before cleaning me up with a washcloth they had hung on the side of the copper water basin.

'Keep him like this, so we can scrub his rear end.' Their voices blended, I did not know who was saying what.

'Here, you take him.'

She passed the cloth quickly over my thighs, her hand wary of touching me.

'Go and put some more water in the pitcher.'

The water seeped out from under the straw mat and trickled to the hole in the threshold of the door, where it flowed out onto the *mastaba*, as would happen when Hajja Khadija washed. But this is filthy, dirty water that must be cleared away as soon as they finish. They washed me with water alone, no soap.

'Splash some more water on him, splash some more.'

I didn't say anything when they splashed the cold water on my back and shoulders. My clothes had been tossed into the path of the water. They weren't any kinder to my body, pulling hard on my head and hands. They pushed my head and back way down between my legs so that they wouldn't have to lean toward my penis. They yanked whatever they wanted to wash towards them. I stayed quiet and kept my head down, surrendering my body, which had come a long way down the road to dying.

'I don't want those two,' I said to my son later that evening, when he came to find me lying half asleep after my washing.

'What did they do?'

'They washed me, the way you wash a corpse. And they put me back in my bed still dirty.'

I recall when I first saw them, I did not avert my eyes from the one leaning into the window, I kept holding onto the window bar. She told her mate in a barking voice that I was awake to try to startle me, to make me look away and take my hand from the window. They had moved to the door, and when they looked in they found me staring right back, my hand firmly on the window bar.

'Have you become cleaner now than before?' one of them asked me, leaning in closer to me, while the other squished the rose into her nose, so that she wouldn't have to inhale my stench.